MELBA ESCOBAR is a fiction writer and a journalist. She lives in Bogotá, Colombia with her children and husband.

ELIZABETH BRYER is a writer and translator from Australia. Her translation of Claudia Salazar Jiménez's *Blood of the Dawn* was published by Deep Vellum in 2016. In 2017 she was a recipient of a PEN/Heim Translation Fund Grant.

Praise for *House of Beauty*:

'*House of Beauty* offers a unique glimpse into modern-day Colombia and an intriguing mystery around issues of gender, class and race, where a woman's worth is too often tied to her beauty, yet her beauty too often gets her in trouble. It's a pleasure to see a story told through the lens of two very different heroines, rare in crime fiction. And, in these times, this novel is also a much-needed critique of everyday misogyny and corruption'

WINNIE M LI, author of *Dark Chapter*

'A tender and revealing tale, written with a delicate touch'

Sunday Times

HOUSE OF BEAUTY

melba escobar de nogales

Translated from the Spanish by
Elizabeth Bryer

4th ESTATE • *London*

4th Estate
An imprint of HarperCollins*Publishers*
1 London Bridge Street
London SE1 9GF

www.4thEstate.co.uk

First published in Great Britain in 2018 by 4th Estate
First published in Colombia by Editorial Planeta Colombiana S. A. in 2015
This 4th Estate paperback edition published in 2019

2

A catalogue record for this book is
available from the British Library

ISBN 978-0-00-826427-7

Printed and bound in Great Britain by
CPI Group (UK) Ltd, Croydon, CRO 4YY

MIX
Paper from
responsible sources
FSC C007454

This book is produced from independently certified FSC paper
to ensure responsible forest management

For more information visit: www.harpercollins.co.uk/green

HOUSE OF BEAUTY

I.

I hate artificial nails in outlandish colours, fake blonde hair, cool silk blouses and diamond earrings at four in the afternoon. Never before have so many women looked like transvestites, or like prostitutes dressing up as good wives.

I hate the perfume they drench themselves in, these women as powdered as cockroaches in a bakery; what's worse, it makes me sneeze. And don't get me started on their accessories – those smartphones swaddled in infantile cases, in fuchsia and similar and covered with sequins, imitation gemstones and ridiculous designs. I hate everything these waxed-eyebrowed, non-biodegradable women represent. I hate their shrill, affected voices; they're like dolls for four-year-olds, little drug-dealer hussies bottled into plastic bodies as stiff as the muscles on a man. It's very confusing; these macho girl-women disturb me, overwhelm me, force me to dwell on all that's broken and ruined in a country like this, where a woman's worth is determined by how ample her buttocks and breasts are, how slender her waist. I hate the stunted men too, reduced to primitive versions of themselves, always looking for a female to mount, to exhibit like a trophy, to trade in or show off as a status symbol among fellow Neanderthals. But just as I hate this Mafioso world, which for the past twenty years or so has dominated the taste and behaviour of thugs, politicians, businessmen and almost anyone who has the slightest connection to power in this country, I also hate the ladies of Bogotá, among whom I count myself, though I do all I can to stand apart.

I hate their habit of using the term 'Indians' to refer to people they consider to be from a low social class. I hate the obsessive need to distinguish between the formal 'usted' and informal 'tú', expecting the servants to address them as 'usted', while they themselves use 'tú'. I loathe the servility of waiters in the restaurants when they rush to attend to customers, saying 'what would you like, sir', 'as you wish, sir', 'on your orders, sir'. I hate so many things in so many ways, things that seem to me unjust, stupid, arbitrary and cruel, and most of all I hate myself for playing my own part in the status quo.

Mine's an ordinary story. It's not worth the trouble of telling in detail. Maybe I should mention that my father was a French immigrant who came to Colombia thanks to a contract to construct a steel mill. My brother and I were born here. Like others of our social class, we grew up behaving as if we were foreigners. Wherever we were – our place in the north of Bogotá, or the apartment in Cartagena's old quarter – we lived our lives surrounded by walls. There were a few summers in Paris, the Rosario

Islands once or twice. My life hasn't been all that different from that of a rich Italian, French or Spanish woman. I learned to eat fresh lobster as a little girl, to catch sea urchins; by the age of twenty-one I could tell a Bordeaux wine from a Burgundy, play the piano and speak French with no accent, and I was as familiar with the history of the Old Continent as I was unfamiliar with my own.

Security has been an issue for me as far back as I can remember. I'm blonde, blue-eyed and 5 foot 8 tall, which is getting less exotic nowadays, but when I was a child it was an ace up my sleeve to win the nuns' affection or to get preferential treatment from my peers. It also attracted attention, and so made my father paranoid about kidnappings. As luck would have it, we were never targeted. Our money and my peaches-and-cream complexion contributed to my isolation, though lately I've begun to wonder if I tell myself that to sidestep the responsibility for being an exile in body and soul. No matter where I've travelled, I've always been someplace else.

At my age, melancholy is part of my inner landscape. Last month I turned fifty-nine. I turn my gaze inward and back on my life far more than I look out to the world around me. Mostly because I'm not interested, and don't like what I find out there. Maybe they're the same thing. I suppose my neurosis has something to do with my scathing reading of the here and now, but it's also inevitable. As Octavio Paz would say, this is the 'house of glances', my house of glances, I have no other. I accept my snobbish nature. I accept, no, more than accept, I embrace my hatreds. Maybe that's the definition of maturity.

When I left Colombia, mothers still made sure their daughters' knees weren't showing; now nothing is left to the imagination. That's another thing that shocked me when I came back. I felt like women's breasts were coming after me with aggressive insolence. At any rate, I haven't managed to readapt to Colombia, and in France I was always a foreigner.

I didn't go to Paris just to study; I was fleeing. I was comfortable there for a long time, I got married, had a daughter, pursued my career. But then the years pressed in on me like thorns and my memories grew hazy, until the day I understood it was time I came back. Divorced, with fifty-seven Aprils under my belt and a twenty-two-year-old daughter studying at the Sorbonne, I packed my life into three old suitcases and made the trip without her. Aline speaks Spanish with an accent and makes mistakes. She's stunning. Slim and very tall, with a preference for women over men that might be fleeting or here to stay. Not that it worries me too much. Though I know that if the poor thing lived here she would have to put up with moralisers, bullying. Things have changed somewhat, it's true. At least now you see a few foreigners in the streets and there are more people who think differently. Even so, aside from my friend Lucía Estrada, with whom I've rekindled my friendship after almost two decades, I'm very alone. Not that I need anyone, not really.

COLOMBIA IS PASSION, according to the poster that greeted me at the airport. And the other day the press reported fifteen dead after a massacre in the south. That passion must be what makes me hate some people so fervently. Señora Urrutia, Señora Pombo and Señora MacAllister, who invite me to take tea and to pray for a sick friend or for the eleven children killed in the latest landslide in the city's south, where they've never set foot. The doormen who take such pleasure in denying everyone entry, the security convoys that charge through the rest of the traffic, the desperate down-and-outs who tear off side mirrors at the traffic lights. Only at work do I connect with my compassionate side. Bitterness hasn't caught up with that part of me yet.

At the start of 2013, I purchased a good apartment on Calle 93, near Chicó Park. I dusted off some corporate shares and bought not just the apartment but also a plot of land in Guasca, where I intend to build a little house in the mountains. In the same apartment, I set up a consulting room and, thanks to my credentials, had patients in no time. I confess I find most of them boring. Their fears are so predictable, and so are all of their complexes, inhibitions and thought processes. Nevertheless, I was short on other hobbies, and fell back on therapy once more. Fortunately, the city has a very broad cultural offering, so every now and then I'm in the mood for a concert or exhibition. I set aside two afternoons a week for such things. Psychoanalysts earn plenty and, given my age and circumstances, I needn't work too much.

In time, I started taking walks on these free afternoons. There's no way of getting to the city centre without spending two hours stuck in traffic, so I keep to my neighbourhood and explore it on foot. On one of these outings I discovered a couple of new bookshops, a splendid pastry place and a few boutiques. Yet I had no desire to try anything on; my body is growing less and less recognisable to me. Often, my own face in the mirror surprises me. My naked legs are an unlikely map, discoloured and forgotten.

It was on one of these strolls around the neighbourhood that, after browsing along Avenida 82, I ended up having a cappuccino and a chocolate soufflé in Michel's Patisserie. I felt guilty, and decided to walk as far as Carrera 15 and then head home, again on foot. After a few blocks, on that clear May afternoon, I paused in front of a white building with glass doors I'd never stepped through. LA CASA DE LA BELLEZA was written in silver lettering. I peeped inside out of simple curiosity. I think it was the name that attracted me. House of Beauty. I was running my eye over the expensive products, for wrinkles, hydration, slimming, stretchmarks and cellulite, when I saw her by the reception desk. She was wearing white tennis shoes and a light-blue uniform and she had her hair pulled up in a ponytail. A long, black tress fell down her back. The rings under her eyes didn't matter, nor did her tired expression: her beauty was forceful, almost indecently so. The young woman oozed life. There was something savage and raw in her that made her seem – how to say it? – real. I'm still not sure if it was the result of discipline and vanity, or simply an inherited gift. I'll never know. Karen is a great mystery. Even more so in a city like this, where everyone's appearance reflects who they are; where their attire, speech and the place they live announce how they will act. The codes of behaviour are as predictable as they are repetitive. I was captivated by her gazelle-like figure, but above all by a certain serenity in her expression. I'd bet she did absolutely nothing to look like that. If I knew anything simply by looking at her, it was that tranquillity has nested in her soul.

Perhaps because I stood there, stunned, staring at her as if she were an apparition, she came forward to ask:

'Do you need help, Señora?'

She smiled effortlessly, as if expressing her gratitude at being alive. I was surprised no one else seemed to perceive her beauty. It was as if the finest orchid had fallen at random into a mud puddle. All around her were women in heels sporting fake smiles. The receptionist was a monstrosity of cherry lips and caked-on blusher. Not her. She seemed to rise above it all, to be the reason for the name of the edifice.

'Yes, thank you. I'd like a wax,' I said, as if I hadn't done my own waxing since I'd had the ability to reason.

'We're not too busy at the moment. Would you like an appointment now?'

'Now's fine,' I said, mesmerised.

'Excuse me, your name?'

'Claire. Claire Dalvard.'

'Please follow me,' she said. And so I followed.

2.

'From a young age, black women straighten their hair with creams, with straighteners, with hairdryers; we chew pills, wrap it up, pin it down, apply hair masks, sleep with stocking caps in place, use a silicone sealer. Having straight hair is as important as wearing a bra, it's an essential part of femininity. A woman's got to do what a woman's got to do, she has to pluck up her courage, use as many clips as it takes. She has to be prepared to endure painful tugging, sometimes for hours on end. It's wasteful and uncomfortable, but there's no getting away from it if you want to achieve the silky straight look,' said Karen in her low, rhythmic cadence.

'And little girls, do they have to do it too?'

'If they're really little, no, but young ladies – eight, nine – then sure, they all straighten their hair, of course,' she said as she removed the wraps.

Karen told me that when she arrived here, she liked the city. And yes. Many find it beautiful. Many are drawn to the mild sadness that distinguishes it, a sadness that is occasionally interrupted by a bright Sunday morning as radiant as it is unexpected.

She left her four-year-old with her mother in Cartagena and came to Bogotá. A former colleague had started up a beauty treatment centre in the Quirigua district, and she offered her a job. She promised her mamá she would send money for Emiliano each month, which she does. Her mamá lives in a house in the San Isidro neighbourhood with Uncle Juan, a confirmed bachelor who is in poor health. They live mainly on her uncle's pension, his due for the thirty years he worked in the post office, and on the money Karen sends.

Karen grew up listening to *vallenato*, *bachata* and, when she was old enough, *champeta*. Her mother, barely sixteen years older than Karen, was crowned Miss San Isidro once, which she thought was a sign she would escape poverty. Instead, she ended up pregnant by a blond guy – a sailor, she assumed – who spoke little Spanish. After love paid Karen's mother that furtive visit, the honey-coloured girl was born, and she shared not only her mother's surname, but her beauty and her poverty too.

Doña Yolanda Valdés sold lottery tickets, sold fried fare, was a domestic worker, bartended in the city. Finally, she devoted herself to her grandson, resigned to her arthritis and to the fact that she gave birth to a girl instead of a boy. At forty years of age she was practically an old woman.

Doña Yolanda's love affairs resulted in two more pregnancies, boys both times, but her luck was such that one was born dead and the other died after just a few days. Yolanda Valdés said the women in her family were cursed. An evil spell fell over them when they least expected it, and condemned them to inescapable solitude.

Karen remembers the seven o'clock Mass on Sundays and waking to the sound of canaries singing. She remembers fish stew at Los Morros beach and taut skin and the dizzying white lights that speckled her field of vision when she floated for a long stretch.

In time, our ritual of shutting ourselves away in that cubicle, sheltered by her youth, the cadence of the sea and the force of her soft, firm hands, became for me a need as ferocious as hunger.

From the moment I first set eyes on her, I wanted to know her. Gently, tenderly, I asked her questions while she moved her fingertips over my back. That's how I found out that she arrived in Bogotá in January 2013, the sunny time of year. First she stayed in Suba, in the Corinto neighbourhood, where a family rented her a small apartment with a bathroom and kitchenette for 300,000 pesos, including utilities. She earned the minimum wage. At the end of the month she didn't have two pesos to rub together, so couldn't send anything home. On top of that, the neighbourhood was unsafe and she lived in constant fear. On the same morning that a drunk man shot two people for blocking a public road during a family get-together, Karen made up her mind to find another place to live.

She moved to Santa Lucía, to the south, near Avenida Caracas, but now had to cross the entire city to reach the salon where she worked.

When a colleague mentioned that an exclusive beauty salon in the north was looking for someone, Karen secured an interview. It was the beginning of April. The city was waterlogged from downpours. Karen had been in the new house barely a couple of weeks and took the deluge as a sign of abundance.

House of Beauty is in Zona Rosa, Bogotá's premier shopping, dining and entertainment district. From the outside, the white edifice suggests an air of cleanliness and sobriety: part dental clinic, part fashionable boutique. Once through the glass doors, you are transported to a land of women. The receptionist behind the counter greets you with her best smile. Several uniformed employees, polished and smiling, are in the display room offering creams, perfumes, eyeshadow and masks in the best brands. On the coffee table in the waiting room are piles of magazines.

Karen remembers arriving on the fifth of April at around 11.30 in the morning. As soon as she crossed the threshold, she breathed deep an aroma of vanilla, almonds, rosewater, polish, shampoo and lavender.

The receptionist, whom she would soon have the chance to get to know better, looked like a porcelain doll. An upturned nose, large eyes and those full, cherry-coloured lips. As she headed past her for the waiting room, Karen wondered what lipstick she used.

At the back, there was a large mirror and two salon chairs where a couple of women did eyebrow waxing, make-up and product testing. They were all wearing light-blue slacks and short-sleeved blouses in the same colour. They looked like nurses, but well-groomed and made up, with impeccably manicured hands and wasp-ish waists. The name badge on one perfectly bronzed woman told Karen her name was Susana.

The cleaner also wore a blue uniform, but in a darker hue. She came over to offer Karen a herbal tea, which Karen accepted. She saw the *tropipop* singer known as Rika come in. She was dark and voluptuous with an enviable tan, possibly older than she looked. She wore sunglasses like a tiara, had a gold ring on each finger and lots of bracelets. Like Karen, she announced herself at the reception desk and then took a seat beside her with a magazine.

'Doña Fina is expecting you, you can go in,' said the receptionist.

'Thank you,' said Karen, making sure to pronounce all her consonants to hide her Caribbean accent.

She went up a spiral staircase, passing by the second floor to reach the third. To her right, three manicure stations, four for eyelashes. In the middle, four cubicles and, at the back, to the left, Doña Josefina de Brigard's office. Karen approached the half-open door and heard a voice beyond it telling her to come in. In the middle of an inviting room, with skylights that revealed a bright morning, stood a woman of uncertain age. She was dressed in low-heeled shoes, khaki pants, a beige blouse and a pearl necklace, with an impeccable blow-dry and subtle make-up.

'Take a seat,' she said in a low voice.

Doña Josefina watched Karen walk to the chair on the other side of the only desk in the room. She looked her up and down with her deep green eyes, raising her eyebrows slightly.

Then she looked straight into Karen's eyes. Karen bowed her head.

'Let me see your hands,' she said.

Karen held them out, a child at primary school all over again. But Doña Josefina didn't get out a ruler to punish her. She let the young woman's hand rest on her own for a moment, then put on her glasses, examined the hand with curiosity, repeated the operation with the left one and asked her once more to take a seat.

She, in contrast, paced around the room. If I had that figure at that age, I wouldn't sit down either, Karen thought.

'Do you know how many years House of Beauty has been running?'

'Twenty?'

'Forty-five. Back then I had three children. I'm a great-grandmother now.'

Karen looked at her waist, delicately cinched by a snakeskin belt. Her pale pink nails. Her almond-shaped eyes. Her prominent cheekbones had something of the opal about them, pale and gleaming. The woman standing before her could have been a film star.

'House of Beauty and my family are all I have. I'm exacting, and I don't make concessions.'

'I understand,' said Karen.

'Yes, honey, you have an I-understand face. You went from an exclusive salon in Cartagena to a run-of-the-mill one in Bogotá. Why?'

'Because I earn more here than there, or at least that's what I thought when I left the coast.'

'It's always about the money.'

'I have a four-year-old.'

'So does every other young woman.'

'A four-year-old?' Karen said.

'I see you've got a sense of humour,' said Doña Josefina, abruptly going back to the formal 'usted'. 'This is a place for serious, discreet women who are willing to work twelve-hour days, who take pride in their work and understand that beauty requires the highest level of professionalism. With your gracefulness, I'm positive you could go far here. You'll see: our clients may have money, some of them a lot of money, but much of the time they are tremendously insecure about their femininity. We all have our fears, and as we start ageing, those fears grow. So, here at House of Beauty we must be excellent at our jobs, but we must also be warm, understanding, and know how to listen.'

'I understand,' said Karen automatically.

'Of course you don't, child. You're not old enough to understand.'

Karen kept quiet.

'So, as I was saying, don't be too quick to answer; if they want to chat, then you chat; if they want to keep quiet, you should never initiate a conversation. Requesting a tip or favours of any nature warrants dismissal. Answering your phone during work hours warrants dismissal. Leaving House of Beauty without seeking prior permission warrants dismissal. Taking home any of the implements without permission warrants dismissal. Holidays are granted after the first year; pension contributions and healthcare are at your own expense. Same with holidays, which are in fact unpaid leave, and can never exceed two weeks, bank holidays included. The files, creams, oils, spatulas and other implements are at your own expense, too.'

'Can I ask what the salary is?'

'That depends. For each service, you receive forty per cent. If you're popular and our clients book a lot of appointments with you, after a few months you could earn one million pesos, including tips.'

'I accept.'

Doña Josefina smiled.

'Not so fast, honey. This afternoon I've got two more interviews.'

Karen found it fascinating that an elegant woman with a well-bred air could switch so easily between being formal and informal.

'Then I would just like to say that I'm very interested,' she said politely.

'We'll have an answer for you in a couple of days.'

As Karen was leaving, Doña Josefina stopped her.

'And one more thing. Who doesn't like a Caribbean accent? Don't try to hide it. No one, not one single soul in this country or any other, likes the way we Bogotans speak.'

A week later, Karen was part of House of Beauty. 'If I had been put in the eyebrow, make-up and eyelashes section, I'd have had trouble competing with Susana,' she told me. Each woman had her strengths, and soon Karen was queen of the second floor. She was assigned cubicle number 3 for facials, massages and waxing. Her beauty, care and professionalism made her a favourite, especially for waxing. She discovered that when Bogotan women came for a Brazilian, it was almost never on their own initiative but because their husband, boyfriend or lover had asked. She told me about her clients and her colleagues at House of Beauty. That was how the name Sabrina Guzmán came up.

Karen knows who has a birthmark on her hip, who suffers from varicose veins, whose breast implants give her trouble, who is about to split up, who has a lover, who is cheating, who is travelling to Miami for the long weekend, who was diagnosed with cancer last week, and who has daily waist-slimming massages without telling her husband.

What's confessed in the cubicle stays in the cubicle, same as happens on the couch. Like the therapist or confessor, the beautician takes a vow of silence. Of course, she would later come to tell *me* things she'd been told in the cubicle. But that was different.

On the treatment table, as on the couch in my line of work, a woman can stretch out in surrender. She obeys the SWITCH OFF YOUR PHONE sign and enters the cubicle ready to disconnect. For fifteen minutes, half an hour, maybe more, she is isolated from the world. She tunes out everything but her body, the silence or the intimate conversation. Often the confidences shared in the cubicle have never been told to anyone before.

Sabrina Guzmán arrived one Thursday in the middle of a downpour, barely half an hour before closing. She reeked of brandy, her hair was soaking wet, and she was in her school uniform. She said her boyfriend was taking her to a romantic dinner and the night would conclude in a five-star hotel. As far as Karen understood, it was the same boyfriend who had wanted to sleep with her on two previous occasions, but hadn't done the honours because, in Sabrina's words, she wasn't as smooth as an apple.

He was coming to Bogotá for two days, so he had to make the most of it. Sabrina didn't explain what he'd be making the most of, but Karen assumed she meant deflowering her. The waxing was torture for them both. Sabrina complained too much, and when Karen saw a few drops of blood, she felt suddenly cold.

When the girl left, Karen stared at that sprinkle of blood on the treatment table cover and wondered how to get rid of it. She tried water, soap and ammonia, but only managed to smudge the stain to a pale rose. That stain would have to accompany her for the rest of her days working at House of Beauty.

3.

A few days later, when Sabrina Guzmán's lifeless body was discovered, the name of Sabrina's lover came back to Karen. The brief write-up said only that the seventeen-year-old, a student at the girls' grammar Gimnasio Feminino, died from an aneurism, and the funeral service would take place at midday the same day, 24 July, at the Church of the Immaculate Conception.

Despite knowing that leaving House of Beauty during work hours was forbidden, Karen felt an urgent need to go. She went into the lavatory, stripped off her uniform, pulled on her skinny jeans and white top, and asked Susana if she could borrow the black blazer she had worn to work that morning.

She went out into the rain with her cheap 5,000-peso umbrella. She forged ahead to the sound of car horns, jumping puddles until she reached Carrera 11, where she boarded a rundown bus. Inside, she folded the umbrella, opened her purse, paid the fare and made her way towards the back, squished between men's warm backsides and the smell of patchouli emanating from women with long hair and dye jobs gone wrong. When she grasped the rail, she thought the same thing she did every time she hopped on a bus: there was nothing more repulsive than the feel of that greasy, sticky metal.

People were still getting on. A fat man's chest pressed against her own. He was so tall she saw his dark double chin above her head when she lifted her gaze.

A child of about eleven hopped on selling mints. He said he had escaped the armed conflict in Tolima. He said he had four siblings. That he was 'head of household'. Karen rummaged in her purse and handed him a 500-peso coin before ringing the bell. The driver stopped abruptly and she leapt to the pavement.

Before going into the church, she stepped inside a department store. She wanted to get rid of the stench from the bus. She applied a test perfume, Chanel No. 5, checked her reflection in a small mirror between rows of blusher pots, fixed her hair, pulled a lipstick from her handbag, applied it carefully and went on her way.

When she got to the church, she moved through the crowd to the front, as if borne along a conveyor belt. In the fourth or fifth pew, she found a free space. Before her was the closed coffin. Very few people would be able to remember the body as she did. Her long, slim toes. Veins showing at the calves. She recalled the freckles on the narrow shoulders, her straight nose, her huge eyes and thin lips, and she suddenly realised Sabrina was beautiful. Her beauty might have been grey, like this city, but at the same time it was subtle, full of secrets.

Sadness washed over her, like a wave in the middle of a calm sea. She clenched her fist to keep from crying, imagined mascara running down her cheeks, and people wondering who the interloper crying her eyes out could be. She thought of the effort the two of them went to just a few days earlier to leave Sabrina as smooth as an apple. Remembering she was in a church, she squirmed. Only then did she glance at the man beside her. She was sure she had seen him before. He was a celebrity. For a moment, she thought she'd seen him on TV presenting celebrity news, but she realised he was too old for that. Then she recognised him. He was the author of the self-help classics *Happiness Is You* and *I Love Myself*.

Karen smiled. Four years ago, before the arrival of her son Emiliano changed her life completely, Karen was in her first semester at the University of Cartagena, studying social work.

What happened to her happened because she was a fool, she knew, though she was not all that less of a fool now; it happened because she was straight-laced, which she still was. And the thing was, the Thinking Skills professor talked so nicely. Yes, he was old, much older than she was – she'd just turned eighteen – but in her eyes, he was learned, enlightened. Professor Nixon Barros had the swagger of Caribbean men. And he talked nicely and had a belly laugh. All that seduced her; whenever she watched him speak, she was hypnotised. Nixon wasn't afraid of tenderness. To Karen, he seemed like a real man. She liked his kinky hair. She liked the sweat that covered his forehead and didn't bother him in the least. She liked his Guayabera shirts, always too big for him, and his cologne.

With Professor Nixon, she explored the Bazurto Market and got drunk for the first time in El Goce Pagano. For almost a year, she skipped classes and kept a secret that made her blush. Karen knew he was married, for the second time, that he lived with a younger wife and a child. But the day he leaned over to kiss her, Karen didn't stop to think about the Prince Charming her mamá had in mind for her, or that Professor Nixon was old, and married – she just closed her eyes and parted her lips.

As the days passed, her happiness, her infatuation, her madness was so acute that she started to let her flesh do the thinking.

She let him make love to her down a dark street in Getsemaní and for the next three or four months kept letting him do so wherever and whenever they could, with growing appetite and surrender. Nixon Abelardo Barros told her so many things that amazed her. For him, she read Melissa Panarello's *100 Strokes of the Brush Before Bed*, Simone de Beauvoir's *The Second Sex*, Coelho's *Love Letters from a Prophet*, and Nietzsche's *Thus Spake Zarathustra*. They kindled a chaotic revolution inside her. That was when she started to look differently at women with waxed eyebrows, and to let the hair grow under her arms as an expression of freedom. 'I wasn't put in this world to please men,' she told her mamá when she asked what those tufts sprouting from her armpits were. 'Come off it, young lady – please me, then.' Doña Yolanda had been known to go without food if money was scarce, yet would never sacrifice her trips to the hairdresser.

Her mother had bet on Karen's beauty as their best shot at escaping poverty. She often told her daughter that if she had been presentable the morning after her fling with the gringo, if he hadn't caught her in a dishevelled mess, with bags under her eyes, he would never have left her waiting in vain, 'whistling iguanas' as she called it. As far as Karen understood, her father was a poet, an artist, a traveller, though she often intuited that her mamá had an active imagination, since from one day to the next he was a troubadour from Sincelejo, a boxer from Turbaco and an English sailor. Karen liked the last idea best.

She was a tall, skinny adolescent, and though her mother fed her as well as she could, the only thing that grew were her bones. Every morning Doña Yolanda readied the grill and cooked up scrambled eggs with cultured buttermilk, rice, beans, yuca and fish, yet the girl only stretched upwards. Happiness for Karen was in that breakfast and berry juice, sitting in the patio, when the *picó* sound systems had been switched off and Calle del Pirata no longer boomed with competing melodies – *vallenato*, *reggaeton*, *champeta*, *rancheras*, the same war every weekend. It was in the barefooted kids kicking up the dust in the street, and in her cousins bringing over crates of chilled Costeñita to drink out the front, some lounging on Rimax chairs, and Uncle Juan in his rocker, always quiet, always serious, his eyes red from getting only a few hours' sleep, his smile helpless as he contemplated her with alcoholic fondness.

In her rebellious period, Karen left untouched the wild curls nature had given her. But after Emiliano was born and she began training as a beautician, the drone of her mother and her beauty-school education wore at her resolve. Not only did she get sick of explaining why she preferred to keep her natural curls, but she became an expert in straight hair.

For her family, girlfriends and people she knew, using a condom when sleeping with a man was the equivalent of being treated like a prostitute. 'If there's love, there's no condom,' Doña Yolanda repeated. She rounded out that sentence with one of her many superstitions: 'If a man tells you he cares for you, look at his pupils. If they dilate, he's lying.' Nixon had said he cared for her, and his pupils had stayed the same. But more than that, Karen trusted him.

Nixon was not another man who talked only about money and cars, and about women as if they were livestock. Nixon didn't go around wearing gold chains, he wasn't obsessed with *champeta* or Rey de Rocha concerts. Nixon liked poetry – like her father, thought Karen, though she didn't really know anything about her father. He also understood that she would choose a university degree any day over competing in the end-of-year district beauty contests.

In that first semester, as well as sitting exams and writing essays, Karen tried marijuana, dancing to classic salsa, but above all she tried sex, whenever and wherever; she discovered she could revert to a primitive state, and she relished it. She learned to go into a kind of trance, almost always with Nixon, and at other times with the help of the Chinese balls her mother kept in the kitchen drawer, Uncle Juan's foot massager or her own hand.

For Karen, reading Eduardo Ramelli's *I Love Myself* meant she could keep any guilt about her behaviour at a prudent distance, or at least distract herself with the arguments of a book underpinned by hedonism. While she was reading it, a few things started happening to her: a sick feeling in the morning, swollen breasts that ached at the slightest touch, sleepiness and fatigue. She was halfway through the book when she decided to take a test one Sunday morning.

'Fuck,' she said. She'd just turned nineteen.

Her mother stopped talking to her for a few weeks, until one suffocating afternoon Karen heard her scooter approaching. Karen was lying on her bed with rollers in her hair, leafing through an old magazine.

'What's the plan? Just lie here all day, getting fat on sunlight?'

'I fed Uncle Juan,' Karen said.

'Go and do something. You're pregnant, not sick. Make yourself busy doing whatever I tell you to, or you're out of here.'

Of all the books she read, the one that stayed with her – the one she read right up to the day she gave birth – was *I Love Myself*, though she no longer thought its message was aimed at her.

The man sitting beside Karen that sunny morning at Sabrina Guzmán's funeral was none other than the author of her bedtime reading, Eduardo Ramelli. He must have been over sixty. His even cinnamon complexion shone, and he had blue eyes and greying, neat hair slicked back with gel, like a heart-throb of old.

'Chanel No. 5,' he whispered in her ear.

Karen kept quiet, not because she didn't know the author of *Happiness Is You* was wearing Paco Rabanne 1 Million, nor because she didn't want to play the game, but because her throat had closed up. Ramelli shot her a half-smile, his eyes fixed on the priest but clearly conscious of her delicate presence beside him.

'What's your name?' he asked after the Eucharist. A long and severe 'shhh' from nearby ended his efforts to get her to talk. Then came the familiar 'Go in peace'. Mass was over. The first two pews were reserved for close family. A woman was crying inconsolably, her arms wrapped tight around a young boy. The keyboard sounded and an out-of-tune choir sang 'Ave Maria' while the funeral goers filed out of the church. Karen reached the aisle and headed for the exit. She smelled Ramelli behind her for a couple of metres, until she lost the scent when two tall women intercepted him. She focused her attention on the ladies. They had fluffy hairdos, like egg whites whisked to stiff peaks. Tailored clothing hung from their brittle bodies. Some had drivers waiting for them outside. Often a bodyguard handed his employer a bulky umbrella at the exit, so she could take her time smoothly skirting the puddles while he ran in the pouring rain to the same car. Then they all got in, women in the back, servants at the front.

Crossing Avenida Calle 100, Karen was assaulted by the beeping horns, the exhaust fumes, the green buses as timeworn as the hunger of those begging, the one-armed men clutching squeegees on the hunt for coins, the displaced people with their dirty bits of cardboard that invariably told the legend of a lost town, the chronicle of a massacre. They'd all used the same black marker to set down the account, with grammatical errors, their handwriting suggesting they'd barely finished third grade, and they'd done so with an unsteady hand, the pavement their only support; once they'd got their story down they set up on the same ordinary corner and went in search of the elusive compassion of the commuters. Several women, almost always black or indigenous, with children hanging from their breasts or back, kept one hand on the little one, held the cardboard in the other and had their coin tins tucked under an arm. It was a sorry balancing act, and the women engaged in it had to be constantly alert to the changing traffic lights.

As soon as the lights turned red, the vehicles were set upon by beggars, criminals, addicts, street performers, down-and-outers, children and pregnant women, as well as disabled, illiterate, displaced, abused and maimed people. The performance was so repetitive and predictable that nowadays no one was the least bit surprised. Or almost no one. Recent arrivals to the cold city were often distressed when confronted with this sight.

The mountains surrounding the city 'marked the limits of civilisation' – at least, that's what students at the elite San Bartolomé College were taught in the seventies. Every day, more people arrived from all over the country. Karen realised with a start that she was just another one of them. She was like the mango sellers, the scrap-metal buyers, the collectors of broken odds and ends, the jugglers and the beggars.

But what astonished her wasn't the vast array of professions that hunger inspired. It was how it had all become routine. She watched those women in their armoured SUVs, the way they wound up the window when someone approached with a hand outstretched. The reaction seemed to come straight out of an instruction manual read in a land where guards, fences and muzzled dogs formed part of the everyday scenery.

When she arrived back at House of Beauty, her legs were tired. Her hands were cold. She ran up to the second floor, and got changed as fast as she could. She was almost ready to go into her cubicle when a sharp knock sounded on the lavatory door.

'Yes?' she said, tying her shoelaces.

'Doña Fina wants to speak to you,' a voice said from the other side.

'Coming,' she said, and checked her reflection in the mirror, fixing her ponytail before going out. This is what happens when you go where you're not invited, she thought. Just when she was starting to save enough money, she was going to get herself fired on account of a client she barely knew. Doña Fina was waiting with the door half-open.

'You wanted to speak to me?'

'Sit down,' Doña Josefina said curtly.

Karen scrutinised her boss. Doña Josefina was raising her left eyebrow slightly.

'Karen, you were absent from work, during work hours, without my consent,' she started. 'I want you to know that nothing escapes me. Even when I'm not here I have eyes and ears everywhere. Do you hear me, honey?'

'Yes, Señora.'

'Now, just so you're aware how much I always know, I'll tell you where you went: to that girl Sabrina Guzmán's funeral. Know how I found out? This morning her mother called, saying she thought she came here often, and that she'd been here the day before last. I wasn't sure who took care of her, so we checked the appointment book. That's how I found out you lost a client. My deepest condolences, honey.'

'I only saw her two or three times.'

'Four, to be exact. And what do you know about her?'

'Not much, Doña Fina, she was a normal teenager.'

'Oh honey, as if that exists. You've got to understand, if they launch an investigation, the police will ask you the same questions. You'd better know how to respond. What did she get done?'

'The usual.'

'A wax?'

'Yes.'

'Bikini?'

'Yes, Señora.'

'The full Brazilian?'

'Yes.'

At that moment, Annie poked her head around the door.

'Sorry to interrupt. Karen, your next client is waiting.'

'Can I leave, Señora?'

'Off you go. But best not mention this to anyone. If you start saying a client died after an appointment with you, no one will set foot in your cubicle again.'

'Thank you,' Karen said, wondering if Doña Fina was serious. She was making sure to pull the door half-shut behind her when she stopped midway and turned around:

'Excuse me, Señora, but the girl is already buried. What could they investigate now?'

'How am I to know?' Doña Josefina waved her hand. 'Now shut that door for me, I have important things to attend to.'

4.

As the years went by, Eduardo cried more easily. He cried in romantic films, on seeing how his hair came away on the pillow, on noting his erectile dysfunction. Not long ago he cried, oh how he cried, when, finally, after a Viagra, and vast amounts of concentration, he managed to be with a woman. The worst thing is, I found out because he himself told me. My only consolation is that, as far as I know, while we were married he never brought them home, or that's what I like to believe. He especially liked a black woman named Gloria, who couldn't have been over twenty. Oh, to have my twenties again, I thought, when I spied them on the terrace of a seafood restaurant on Calle 77. It was a coincidence. I had been to see a dermatologist, and decided to walk home. I saw them from the pavement opposite. He squeezed and released her hand in a seductive move so old that, back in the day, it worked its magic on me. I knew her name because once, when I was using his computer, I opened a folder called 'Gloria', where I saw the photos. As with other times, I didn't say anything. I couldn't blame him for going out on the street to get what I'd stopped giving him so long ago. I was hurt more by his selfishness, his lack of interest in me and the fact that he left me on my own. The girl got to me less. Over the years, bit by bit I'd lost all feelings of desire, and this got worse with the onset of menopause. I thought, if he needs sex, he can go get it where it's on offer. But he could at least keep me company, show interest in the things I care about. Though, truth be told, I'm not too sure what these are any more, since I've been focused on him for so many years.

That day, when I saw them with their hands entwined, brushing against a shrimp ceviche cocktail, I'd just been diagnosed with vitiligo. Just what I needed, I thought. I held in the urge to cry in front of that cardboard cut-out of a doctor. He was looking at me with such pity. But he was only a whippersnapper, he couldn't have been over thirty.

I went out quiet, calm. Said to myself, I'm going to walk home, I'll go via the supermarket. The diagnosis explained the large white streak that had appeared a few months ago, ruining my black hair. Same went for the patches on my ankle and left cheek. I was feeling low, I won't deny it. And right then I came across my husband with that ebony sculpture, the woman I'd already seen in her birthday suit. It was too much. One humiliation after another. And the worst thing was, I didn't even care. I'm not sure what it is. Whether it's the menopause or just that I've grown used to living with shame, the fact is I remained in a listless state I thought I'd never come out of, until Claire came back into my life.

She gave me back some of the energy I'd lost. We hadn't been especially close at school. As a psychologist, my father was respectable more than wealthy, so we lived in different worlds. Claire was beautiful, haughty, proud. She was from a good family and was outstanding at whatever she set her mind to; I was nothing special. On top of that, I had frightful mousy hair with about as much lustre as potato soup, and horrendous glasses. We had a friend in common, Teresa, who these days is wife of the Minister for Internal Affairs. But Claire was a sophisticated woman from a very different world from me.

Nevertheless, when we met up for the first time after she'd said she was back in Colombia, she was so affectionate, and I suspected she was lonely. So, we caught up a second time, four or five days ago, and drank an outrageous amount of whisky. I confess I'd never had a whisky in my life. I'd tried it, so I knew what it tasted like, but I'd never drunk a whole one. When I had the chance, I drank a glass of wine, maybe a champagne or Baileys. Never whisky. But Claire poured herself one and said, 'Do you want a whisky?'

I wasn't about to say 'Do you have a Baileys in the cupboard somewhere?' like an old lady or a fifteen-year-old. No. I summoned the courage and said, 'Yes, pour me one, yum.'

Recalling it now makes me chuckle. The first one tasted awful, but the next ones were a riot. That's the kind of thing that happens when I'm with Claire. It's like, let's see, we're the same age – I think I might even be a little younger – but next to her I feel so straight-laced. In contrast, she's independent, liberated. Youth is definitely a mindset. On top of that, she's heading towards sixty and is still stunning, absolutely stunning.

So, getting back to Eduardo, I met him when I was twenty-five. According to him this meant that, as a woman, I was in the prime of my life. He was thirty-seven. Until then I'd been a bookworm. My mother died when I was eleven. I was always quite ugly. In any case, I was never a beauty. I didn't know much about men, and what I knew about relationships came from books. I decided to become a psychoanalyst because I grew up listening to my father talk about his cases, so it seemed the most natural thing to do. I don't believe I even considered other options, though now I think I should have studied biology.

And so I met Eduardo at a conference. He seemed relaxed. Later I'd think frivolous. He seemed sure of himself, as though he had no need to impress anyone, though with time I'd come to interpret this as narcissism. While narcissism is a natural part of the human make-up, whereby any discovery that refutes one's self-image is rejected, Eduardo takes this to the limit. He verges on sociopathy, a diagnosis that has taken me almost thirty years to arrive at. At least I devoted myself to writing and not to my patients. It's possible the poor things have had a terrible time with me, since it takes me years to arrive at a diagnosis. But anyway. Speed has never been my thing. I was struck by the fact that a fine-looking man like Eduardo would notice me. I've always been full-bosomed, maybe that's what attracted him. That and the manuscript, or the fact that I was always very understanding and maternal with him. I still remember the time he called me 'mami'. He was distracted, leafing through the newspaper; I asked him something – whether he'd booked an appointment with the urologist, something like that – and, not lifting his gaze, he said, 'No, mami,' and then went bright red with embarrassment. I burst out laughing.

We got married a year after we met. I'd only been with one man before him, in a relationship as strange as it was uncomfortable for the both of us. I was head over heels for Eduardo. I couldn't believe such a dish had looked twice at a woman like me. And as well as being good-looking, he was fun, witty, self-assured, worldly, classy – in other words, everything I wasn't. As something of a dowry, you could say, I offered him a manuscript, which he published to great success. It was a book about the kind of love that kills. He thought it was extraordinary and only proposed a few changes. He published it under his own name, and mine – Lucía Estrada – wasn't mentioned anywhere. I must have been spellbound by Eduardo because it's not that I didn't care; it actually made me proud. All I could think was, *He liked it so much he published it under his own name*. I couldn't believe it. And then I wrote another book, which he again published under his name, but this time I'd said, 'Look, my love, truth is I'm no good at giving interviews, at responding to emails, at explaining the theories put forward here. So, if you want, you keep signing your name.'

And to my surprise he'd said he'd be happy to. I was sort of hoping he would say, 'No, my love, you can do it, you deserve the recognition, how could you think I'd sign for you.' But that's not what happened. Three decades and sixteen books later, Eduardo is the second-most-prominent self-help author in South America. And we all know who the number one is.

At the start of our marriage, having a child was up for discussion. He hadn't closed the door and I thought that he'd keep it open for me. But no. He didn't want children. Nor did he want to live abroad, because here he had his fans and his business associates. I kept writing the books. That, at least, took me to all different places. He gave talks, I wrote. He signed books, I wrote. He went shopping, I wrote. He spent the weekend with a lover, I wrote. And that's how it went for thirty-three years. It's not like I've really suffered or anything. I've lived comfortably. I like books; I feel secure, calm around them. I've had a good life. Plus, I loved Eduardo so much that his happiness was also mine. And we had things in common, though in all honesty he didn't much like talking about books. Actually, I'm not certain what bonded us, exactly – cooking, maybe, as he knew how to make three or four dishes, and when he cooked he talked to me about what he was doing. I'm not sure what we did together all those years, but I didn't feel bitter, or unhappy. None of that. It was only when we separated that I came to a diagnosis: the neurotic patient, in this case Eduardo, fashions his world into a mirror, and expects a response that reflects his own expectations about himself. In other words, the patient sees his wife, his friends and his work as projections, his idealisations of what they should be. In this way, he doesn't recognise the other as an independent being, because the other only exists as a reflection of his own unsatisfied needs. When the inevitable failure of an idealised expectation occurs, an irreversible frustration overcomes him, giving rise to the process that Freud, following Jung, calls 'the regression of libido'. This is how I lived for three decades with a man who never knew me nor wanted to get to know me.

He was a man for whom the important thing was feeling loved, admired and respected by an anonymous but irrefutable mass. My existence was important to him only in that it continued to validate his sense of self.

The fact is, in my own way, I was happy. I suppose that my happiness consisted in the 'negation of my own desires', in 'renouncing myself' and even in 'self-punishment': Claire's words. I served him well, in all senses of the word. The ironic thing is, I still serve him. Before finalising a divorce settlement, I moved to a small apartment in La Soledad, where I still write books for

Eduardo, in exchange for a monthly allowance and the occasional furtive encounter, almost always infelicitous. He still seems to me drop-dead gorgeous, and funny, and so refined; he's as adorable as they come. Though, as I said, I haven't felt desire for a long time. The point is that Eduardo suffered a lot as a child. His father mistreated him, and he had to learn to put up defences, to protect himself. We shouldn't be so quick to judge others. And that's what I told Claire. No one is as good or bad as he or she seems. Eduardo was never a bad man. Although, there's some truth to the idea that I became more and more a mother figure. Yes, a mother figure. I brought him his slippers. Made him coffee. Ran his bath. And he turned to me for comfort, for reassurance. My poor Edu.

The last time we saw each other, he tried to kiss me. We'd been to dinner at a new restaurant. He brought me home and asked if he might have a drink before he left.

'I'm tired,' I said, trying to get out of it.

'Just one glass, my Lu-chia.'

One glass turned into the five or six that were in the bottle and a never-ending monologue. I nodded off at the other end of the sofa. Eduardo wanted to talk about his impotence, then leaned over to kiss me, and I pushed him away.

'I can't, my love, I'm sorry,' I mustered the energy to tell him.

'You can't or you can't be bothered?' he asked, lighting a cigarette, not looking at me.

In the cold early hours of 23 July, he woke on the couch. I had settled a blanket over him before going to bed. I fell asleep at almost three in the morning and two hours later heard him. But what was he doing? I wondered this in a half-awake state, because I could hear him tripping and moving about in the little living room while murmuring into his phone. A loud thud got me out of bed. I went out to see what was happening. Eduardo was searching for his shoes in a rush. The living room was still in semi-darkness. He had knocked over the bottle of whisky and the little that remained had spilled onto the parquetry floor.

'What's wrong?' I asked, alarmed.

'I'm sorry, Lucía, I have to go.'

'So early?'

'A friend's in trouble, he needs my help, I'll tell you about it later.'

Eduardo left. Right away I emptied the ashtray of my ex-husband's butts. I wondered how it was that someone over sixty could have a friend in trouble at this time of the morning. It could happen in adolescence, but at this age? It reminded me why I left him. Eduardo was self-ish and, forgive me, thought more with his willy than his head. How I hated the smell of cigarettes. One of the good things about my new place was that no one smoked here. That, and the silence, the peace. I bought a yoga book for beginners, a special mat and a few candles. Eduardo made fun of me. He thought it ridiculous that at this stage of my life I wanted to learn something new. Every afternoon I dedicated an hour to it, and bit by bit improved. The simple fact that I didn't have to accompany Eduardo on his trips any more gave me lots of freedom. One or two afternoons a week, I went to the cinema, sometimes for long walks down Park Way. I even thought about getting a dog.

I got out a slice of bread and slotted it into the toaster. Mopped the parquetry floor. The smell of whisky nauseated me. I opened the windows. Prepared a coffee, watered the plants and brought the laptop to the dining table to go over what I'd written the day before. I served up the toast and coffee, put my glasses on and started to read: 'This is how infidelity becomes the most common reason behind divorce and marital maltreatment. It can cause depression, anxiety, loss of self-love and many other psychological disturbances, representing the dark side of love.' I read it twice. It made me laugh. I couldn't read it again. *The Dark Side of Love* could be describing the two of us. I felt listless. What would happen if I didn't write the book? The royalties from the others would be enough for us to live off. True, there was an existing contract for *The Dark Side of Love* and it was scheduled for release next year. But Eduardo could always find another ghost writer: nowadays there were a lot of decent young writers around, and some of them had studied psychology.

And he seemed to be doing very nicely from the business he had going with his associate. It wouldn't matter in the least if we didn't publish a book; it wasn't as though we would starve. Though Eduardo was becoming increasingly ambitious. Greedy, you could say. In fact, that had been another catalyst for our separation. His plans to buy a place in New Hope, on top of the Gloria incident, were the last straw. It didn't matter how much I criticised New Hope's flashy Miami look, with all its showy pride at being the most expensive postcode in Bogotá. He'd insisted that we would be comfortable living among 'people like us'.

'People like us? And at what point did you become a prototypical, snobbish Colombian?'

'Don't start with me, Lucía,' he'd said. 'Anyone would think you were penniless.'

The conversation hadn't lasted much longer. He argued that there was nothing wrong with wanting the best.

'We deserve it, my Piccolina,' he'd said.

He'd pulled out a green folder from his leather briefcase then opened it slowly and pulled out some papers.

'Piccolina, the matter is already settled. All you need to do is sign here, and we'll have made the best investment of our life.'

Eduardo leafed through the papers and started reading out loud and telling me about the property. 'You have to see the vertical garden on the rocks out the back. There are 350 car spaces, a security room, 48 security cameras.'

He kept reading. 'You'll love the function room, my love, it has its own kitchen. And amazing furniture – all designer, very tasteful. But the best part is the clubhouse. You like swimming, you'll love it. There's a climatised semi-Olympic pool, with a swimming instructor, sauna, steam room, Pilates room ...'

The phrase 'you like swimming' had echoed in my ears. The truth was, I did. I had liked swimming as an adolescent, and I had at university, too. Why had I stopped swimming? 'You like swimming' echoed in my head again and again until I felt like I was drowning.

I also liked Joan Baez and Simon and Garfunkel, I liked heading to the mountains on weekends, I liked preparing *ajiaco* soup – but Eduardo didn't eat *ajiaco*, didn't like my music, and if he left Bogotá it had to be by plane. So, I'd adapted my preferences to suit his, and I'd adapted so much I'd become blurry. He finished talking and, not noticing my red eyes or my silence, he put the papers back into his briefcase, changed his jacket and dabbed on some cologne.

'Goodbye, my love,' I said with a smile from the bed.

'Don't eat too much,' he said.

I got into bed with a bag of potato chips and a box of chocolates. By midnight I'd watched an episode of *CSI* and two of *Mad Men*, and I was tired. The women in those series are heroines, I thought, but, in the end, it never does them any good. Eduardo still hadn't come home. My eyes were swollen from crying.

When I turned off the TV I imagined sleeping in another bed. A smaller one, but my own. I fell asleep thinking about a window overlooking the street, hope-fully alongside a park, an open-plan kitchen, a few plants, a round dining table and a little lamp hanging above it. Eduardo came back when dawn was breaking. I was up and sitting in front of the computer, looking for apartments in La Soledad.

'Up working so early?' he'd said.

'What do you think?' I'd said, determined to find the perfect place for myself, the room of my own where there would be no space for him.

And now I was in that place of my own, collecting his cigarette butts. When I finished cleaning, I decided to ask Claire if we could make a habit of catching up once a week. I decided not to let him smoke at my place again. I raised the calendar and marked the date: 23 July. From this day forward, no one smokes in here, I said to myself, circling the date with the same red pen that I used to correct drafts of his books.

5.

S abrina was in her uniform. That's why they didn't let her into the hotel bar where she was meant to be going on her date with Luis Armando. She would have liked to go for a drink, or for him to take her to a restaurant, or at least to go for a walk. But he insisted on seeing her in his room.

'I can't wait to cover you in kisses,' he said.

And that phrase was enough for Sabrina to feel her heartbeat quicken.

'Do you love me?' he asked in the voice that often murmured over the telephone how much he wanted her.

'A lot,' Sabrina said, turning red. It was the first time a man other than her father had asked.

When she went up to his room, she saw that Luis Armando was drunk. She was drunk, too, from the brandies she tossed back earlier so that she could bear the pain of the waxing. If she'd been sober, perhaps she would have reacted faster. But she wasn't. She realised that coming here hadn't been a good idea. Nevertheless, instead of leaving, she stared into his eyes, searching for the spark of love she thought she'd detected in them once. She was ready to become a woman.

6.

W hen she left her boss's office, Karen felt the women's eyes on her. The three in the eyelashes section looked up from the faces before them and scrutinised her. Even the woman distributing coffees turned to stare. Karen imagined that if they didn't have clients right then, they would interrogate her. What was it? Did all of them know that Sabrina Guzmán had died, and that she'd been Karen's client?

She went downstairs to give Susana her jacket before she went back to her cubicle. Susana was immersed in whatever she was typing into her phone, which she hid as soon as she saw Karen.

'Thank you,' Karen said, handing her the jacket.

'No problem, gorgeous,' Susana said with a smile.

Karen noticed the handbag at her feet and wondered if it was original.

'Yes, it's real,' said Susana, who apparently had the power to read minds.

'It's lovely.'

'Thank you, gorgeous!' said Susana. 'You seem nice. Save my number, you never know when you might need a friend. There are some green-eyed, catty little minxes round here – they've been known to get their claws out,' she added in an almost whisper.

Susana got out her phone to call Karen and, while she typed in her number, Karen noticed she had the latest iPhone. A tablet was peeking from her handbag.

'Why do you bring that handbag to work, to make them jealous?' asked Karen.

'Yes, that too.'

Annie interrupted to tell Karen her next client had arrived.

'Don't you worry about the minxes,' said Karen. It was the first time she'd used that word to refer to their House of Beauty colleagues. 'They'd never have the money for a tablet like that.'

'Oh, gorgeous,' said Susana, 'It's so obvious you're new. If they had to stop eating they would, if it meant they didn't have to miss out. Anyway, if you ever need a lend of the handbag, or some clothes, just let me know.'

Karen went up to the second floor thinking that Susana seemed like a good person. Once in the cubicle, she lit the wax warmer. There were two knocks at the door. Before opening up, she called Annie at reception and asked who to expect.

'You really don't know?' she answered on the other end before hanging up.

Fortunately, Karen remembered her name when the door opened. Even if she hadn't seen her before, she would have recognised her from the celebrity news, which she presented in the evenings.

Karen admired the TV presenter. She had put out of her mind that she'd treated her badly on two or three previous occasions. She was even more beautiful in real life than she was on TV. Karen loved her straight hair.

'Doña Karen, how is life treating you?' Karen asked cheerfully.

Doña Karen didn't hear her, or didn't want to answer.

'You can pop your clothes on this chair, I'll leave you a moment so you can change. Are you here today for a bikini wax? Do you need the disposable briefs?'

'No, only legs and underarms.'

'All right, Doña Karen, in that case you can leave your underwear on. I'll be with you in just a moment. Would you like a coffee? Or a herbal tea?'

'A herbal tea would be nice.'

She requested a herbal tea to cubicle 3, then searched the cupboard for an electric blanket. There it was. If anything from the central closet went missing, everyone's pay was docked. She returned to the cubicle where Doña Karen was lying on the treatment table. Doña Karen was thirty years old and had been coming to House of Beauty for years. Another worker had always looked after her, until one day Doña Karen's phone went missing and the worker was dismissed, even though there was no proof or inquiry. That's how twenty years at House of Beauty had ended for Karen's predecessor, and how the crown jewel had been placed in Karen's hands.

'Karen's your name, isn't it?'

'Yes, Señora.'

'It's a bit uncomfortable for me, the two of us having the same name, you know?'

'How so, Señora?'

'Drop the "Señora", I'm not married. Let's see. How can I get across that we can't have the same name? Should I draw a diagram? "Hello, Karen, how are you?" "Fine, and you, Karen?" "Fine, Karen." Get what I'm saying, now?' said Doña Karen while Karen passed a tissue daubed with cleansing cream over her skin.

'Would you like a numbing cream, or will you be fine just like that?' asked Karen.

'But are you listening to what I'm saying?' said Doña Karen, irritated. 'You've got to have a middle name, right? Or can I give you a nickname?'

'If you like, Doña Karen. I don't have a middle name.'

'Is the concept really so difficult for you to grasp?'

As she dusted Doña Karen's calves with talcum powder, Karen took the wooden spatula and tested the temperature of the wax on the back of her left hand. Doing this always reminded her of testing Emiliano's bottles to make sure they weren't too hot. She thought Doña Karen must be having a bad day. After all, it couldn't be easy being famous. No doubt people hounded her on the street asking for autographs, and it had to be tiring being on everyone's lips. She used the spatula to spread wax over Doña Karen's legs up to the knees. Then she cut a strip of cloth, which she pressed against her skin before ripping it off in one go. Her client let out a whimper.

Karen remembered the time a client at another salon filmed Doña Karen making a scene during a pedicure because they'd cut a toenail too short. It was rumoured this was why no one could have phones inside the cubicles, so workers couldn't take photos or videos of clients that might lead to House of Beauty facing a lawsuit.

'We'll be finished in a sec. Would you like the blanket?' Doña Karen nodded.

'Now we'll move on to underarms, and then we'll be done,' said Karen, softly massaging aloe vera into her legs.

Karen thought that whoever had secretly filmed the video was a bad person. It wasn't right to benefit from others' misfortune, she told herself as she admired the smoothness of Doña Karen's skin.

'I know,' said Doña Karen suddenly, pulling Karen out of her musings, 'Pocahontas!' She laughed maliciously. 'Adorable, isn't it? It suits you perfectly, with your black hair, those eyes and your big lips. You must be part-Indian, are you?' She started laughing hysterically.

'If you want to call me Pocahontas, that's fine by me,' said Karen, as she started over: she cleansed the surface to be waxed, tested the wax temperature, dusted on talcum powder, spread numbing cream, applied the wax with the wooden spatula, ripped it off with a cloth strip and massaged in aloe vera. Doña Karen had her eyes closed most of the time, but there was a faint smile on her face. Karen wondered if the smile was always there or if she was faking it for her. In actual fact, Karen Marcela Ardila – as she *did* have a middle name – had had a smile stuck to her face since she was crowned Little Miss Colombia at the age of eight. She'd been so persistent with the expression that now it was difficult to control. She smiled all the time, even in sad or dramatic situations, which was another reason she could never present anything but the celebrity news.

Doña Karen's implants looked like they were threatening to burst. She had a curvaceous body and liked to show it off, not only in the underwear catalogues. She was wearing a lace thong and a size 30G black silk bra. She had a caramel skin tone, her hair was a reddish champagne and she had a tiny nose. It was as if the features of a Walt Disney princess had been superimposed onto the body of a Playboy bunny.

'We're done,' said Karen in relief.

Doña Karen got down off the treatment table, her smile fixed firmly in place. She swayed her huge backside from one side to the other like a peacock in courtship. Karen was handing her a bathrobe when the cubicle phone sounded.

'Your next appointment has arrived, this time don't ask who,' Annie said and hung up.

Karen didn't remember.

'You can get changed while I go downstairs to get your receipt ready,' she said.

'Thank you, Pocahontas,' Doña Karen said, not looking at her, still smiling. 'Your beauty's so savage, you know. You're like a little Indian girl in a loincloth.' She let out a childlike, shrill laugh. 'Though that hair of yours has been straightened, hasn't it?'

Karen didn't answer.

Doña Karen gave her a 1,000-peso tip, not enough for even a bus fare. She also paid 1.5 million pesos – double Karen's monthly earnings until a few weeks ago – to buy herself a couple of creams, a Sisley and an Olay. Out of everything that happened, the thing Karen found most offensive was that 1,000-peso note.

Karen hid her tips under her mattress, where she had more than a million pesos now. Once she had 2 million, she would bring Emiliano here. It was enough to pay for his food, schooling, and someone to take care of him while she was at work, at least for a few months. She would save up the rest of the money by doing home visits, getting a Sunday job – whatever was necessary. At this rate, it would be three more months. It wasn't such a long time, she consoled herself.

She was going back up the stairs when she heard Doña Karen's voice:

'Pocahontas!'

She turned around.

'How!' she said, emulating a greeting she'd heard in a Hollywood Western.

Karen stared at her. This time she was the one faking a smile. The TV presenter had called her an Indian in front of everyone, in revenge for the fact that she had the same name. She could feel everyone's eyes latching onto her like leeches. She could hear their treacherous giggles; they were like Cinderella's stepsisters. Minxes, she said to herself. Luckily, Susana came to her rescue:

'Wow, you must have won over Karen Adila if she's given you a pet name already!'

And she kept walking.

Karen was relieved to have at least one ally. She didn't know what her reasons were, only that Susana had decided to protect her. She hadn't reached the door of her cubicle when she bumped into a middle-aged woman with poorly dyed hair, long legs and too much make-up. She still wasn't sure where she'd seen her face before when the woman took her by the arm.

'Are you Karen?'

'Yes, Señora, how can I help you?'

'I'm Consuelo, Sabrina Guzmán's mother. Do you remember her?'

The image of a weeping mother with her arms around a small boy at the funeral a few hours before came to Karen's mind.

'Did you book an appointment with me?' she asked nervously.

'Yes,' the woman said.

'Come through, please,' Karen said, guiding her towards the cubicle. 'And what would you like done?'

'Me? Nothing. Charge me something, if you like, but I only came to talk to you.'

'Would you like a coffee or a herbal tea?'

'I don't want anything,' she said, her eyes fixed on the treatment table. Karen went to fetch her a glass of water, more to leave the cubicle a moment and not have to look at her than because she thought she needed one. When she came back, the woman was sliding down the wall. Sobs were racking her body. She'll end up on the floor, Karen said to herself, and she did. She crouched down before Consuelo. She was going to ask her to get up, but at the last moment she had a change of heart. The mother in her made her put an arm around her shoulders. The woman cried. Who knows how long they were bent over like that? Then, in an instant, she stopped. Her face was wet, her make-up running. She looked terrible.

'Are you sure you don't want a treatment?' asked Karen. 'I'm not sure what else I can offer you. What would you like: a massage, a deep skin hydration?'

'A massage,' the woman said, to put a stop to her persistence.

'All right, we'll concentrate on the back muscles and, if you have any pain or knots, let me know and we'll work on them, how does that sound?'

'I just want you to tell me about my daughter.'

Karen was troubled by that request.

'Your daughter didn't say much, Señora. If you'd like, you can get undressed. Just leave on your underpants,' she said as she put on some music.

'Did you wax her?'

'Yes, I did, Señora.'

'You did a good job. She looked like a doll,' said the girl's mother, undoing her bra.

'Thank you,' said Karen, thinking this was the strangest conversation she'd had in her life. 'Now lie down on the treatment table, I'm going to put an electric blanket over you so you don't get cold. Just a minute. Almond or lavender oil?'

'I told you I didn't come for this,' the girl's mother said again, her tone betraying a slight irritation. 'And why else would my girl get a wax, if not for a date? I know she was seeing someone but she never told me anything. I don't even know his name.'

Karen didn't answer. Instead, she massaged the woman's temples, her head, her neck. She was going to continue with her arms, but, when her gaze rested on the running make-up, she couldn't fight the impulse to correct it. She daubed a tissue with make-up remover and passed it over her face, then applied a cleansing gel and finally a moisturiser.

She continued massaging her arms and, when she reached her left hand, Sabrina Guzmán's mother started crying again. From then on, she wept softly while Karen worked.

After twenty minutes, she asked her to lie face down and only then, on turning over, did the woman ask:

'Do you have children?'

'A four-year-old boy.'

Karen worked on her back for a long time. It was full of knots.

'And they want me to believe it was suicide ...' she said out of nowhere.

'Suicide, Señora? I thought it was a natural death, an aneurysm.'

'That's what's in the newspapers, what did you expect?'

Karen kept quiet.

'And now my girl is dead and buried, what am I going to do? My God! What am I going to do?'

She'd erupted into a grief-stricken wail. Karen had to stop the massage.

'Have you spoken to the police?'

'They keep telling me that as long as the medical report states an overdose of Tryptanol as cause of death, there are no grounds for opening an investigation.'

'Tryptanol?'

'A drug, an anti-depressant that you can overdose on. What do you know, Karen?' she asked again.

'She didn't look like someone who wanted to kill herself. How did she commit suicide, or how do they say she did?'

'At the San Blas Hospital, they said a taxi driver dropped her. He said he picked her up on the corner of Calle 77 and Carrera 9, at around five in the morning. He said she asked to be taken to San Blas Hospital as fast as possible, that it was an emergency. And when he got there, she wouldn't wake up. So he got out to take a look at her, and saw she had a packet of Tryptanol in her hand. He opened it and, inside, a whole blister was empty.'

'So she'd swallowed the pills?'

'That's what the medical report says.'

'But was an autopsy done? Was the taxi driver called to testify?'

Sabrina's mother continued to cry, but quietly now.

'I was scared. At the time, I was thinking the priority was to have her buried on hallowed ground. Did you know suicides aren't admitted into God's kingdom?'

Karen touched her right foot and Consuelo Paredes let out a sigh and closed her eyes. Karen rubbed the insteps with a little cream. Then she rotated her feet in one direction, and in the other. She rolled her fist around on the sole of her foot, first up and down, then in circles.

'I don't know what to say. Maybe it wasn't suicide. Maybe ...'

Right then, the phone rang. Karen had no option but to answer.

'Just a moment, Señora. Yes, Annie?'

Karen had to cut short her time with Sabrina Guzmán's mother.

'I'm so sorry, Señora, our time is up. I have another client, she's coming up as we speak.'

She got dressed quickly. Before leaving she gave Karen a hug, pressed a business card into her hand that read *Consuelo Paredes*, *Real Estate Agent* and listed her phone numbers.

Two knocks on the door announced Rosario Trujillo.

'How are things?' she said on entering, not looking anywhere. 'I'd like a slimming treatment on my waist and thighs, and then an eyebrow touch-up, okay?'

She insisted on slimming down, even though she was underweight.

'My pleasure, Señora,' Karen said, and went out to find the warm gel, rollers and ultrasound.

When she came back, Rosario Trujillo was lying on the treatment table talking into her phone. As soon as Karen entered, she switched to English. Karen had begun to get used to that, too.

In the end, she was so irritated she switched back to Spanish and Spanglish, shrieking at her husband:

'I'm not going on Indian Airlines! Put me in first class, or you're going alone with the kids.'

As soon as she hung up, Señora Rosario started complaining. First, she complained about the heat, then about the voltage, then about the lack of ventilation in the cubicle and the short amount of time they had together, about the housekeeper who had quit without warning, about how her daughter no longer spent much time with her, about the traffic, about the poor water quality and once more about the heat. The hour went by slowly.

Karen wondered why no one told Señora Rosario that her low weight was becoming a worry, that she definitely didn't need to slim down. She was tempted to say as much, but chose to keep her job instead.

'We're done,' said Karen finally.

Then she went out to get the bill ready while Señora Rosario got dressed. It was barely five o'clock. She still had three hours to go before she could leave. Though Señora Rosario could be exasperating, she left Karen a 10,000-peso tip. Karen was grateful for that. On hurrying down the stairs, Karen saw Señora Trujillo's bodyguard. The minxes' gossip had it that she was married to an important politician. When she took the bill to the cash register she felt like she was being watched again. She was getting ready to go upstairs with Doña Rosario's receipt when her next appointment stopped her with a light touch on the shoulder.

'If you're really busy, don't rush, I'll wait here until you're ready.'

Karen turned and looked into my eyes.

'Doña Claire, it's lovely to see you. Give me a moment and I'll come down for you.'

After saying this, she rested her hand on my shoulder for a second.

Since the fateful day when I stepped through House of Beauty's doors, I'd come back often. I always asked for Karen, and if she wasn't available I chose to come back some other time rather than let another woman touch me. I felt so comfortable in her presence. I could lie down on the white, warm towels, surrender to the silence, close my eyes, drift off.

Karen told me about Sabrina and her unexpected death. She also told me about the girl's mother, about having to interrupt her in the middle of her outpouring because of her four o'clock appointment. I listened to her, maybe because the therapist in me couldn't help it, maybe because I was truly interested, but either way, I listened.

'Do you think it was suicide?'

'I don't know.'

'Is there anything you do know?'

'She was going to see her boyfriend.'

'Interesting. How old would he be?'

'I don't know. She never said, but he's a young professional, perhaps twenty-seven, thirty at most.' Karen told me other details she remembered: where he worked, his first name. 'But why didn't I tell her mother what I knew?'

'Maybe it's intuition, maybe you're protecting yourself. Or maybe you're respecting the confidentiality of your conversations with the girl. In any case, it's a respectable decision.'

I realised we were up to the revitalising exfoliant with olive-stone grains, which had to be left on the skin for six minutes. Time had flown.

'Doña Claire, don't speak for the next six minutes, until I remove the exfoliant.'

'You talk, then.'

'What about?'

'Whatever you like. And Karen, drop the "Doña", please.'

For those six minutes, Karen spoke about Nixon Barros, her son's father; about Emiliano, Rosario Trujillo and Karen Ardila; about her calculations to reach the end of the month. She told me about Ramelli's *I Love Myself*, and the importance of being on the lookout for signs from the angels, who are always with us. In those six minutes, I knew Karen was the protagonist of a story that was already forming in my head.

'Now give me a massage.'

'Now?' Karen asked, surprised.

'Yes,' I said, trying to appear casual. I wasn't sure what strange force was making me stay by her side. I didn't want to go. I wanted to stay put, my eyes closed, feeling the touch of her hands and sensing her breath.

'Let me check if I have another appointment and, if not, it would be a pleasure.'

When she hung up the phone, she said: 'I can give you a massage. Would you like some disposable briefs or are you fine with the ones you have on?'

'I'm fine like this,' I said, feeling a faint embarrassment. I got undressed with my back to Karen. In any case, it was dim in the cubicle. Now her hands weren't on my face or neck. They were everywhere, even on my ankles, on the soles of my feet.

'Would you like to hear the sea?' she asked.

I couldn't answer. I pretended I was asleep. Karen put the sounds of the sea in stereo and came back to my calves. I'd never dedicated a single thought to them, yet now they seemed to contain the world.

'Do you exercise?' she asked.

I smiled.

'I was sporty years ago, now I barely go for walks.'

Her hands travelled over my legs, my abdomen. The scent of coconut filled the cubicle and waves broke against the door that was pushed shut against the real world. I didn't want to go back there, I wanted to stay like this forever, with Karen, with her scent of flowers, her child's laugh, her seriousness whenever she spoke. Karen talked and I could sense only my body, in sync with the universe, pulsating. I couldn't remember anyone ever touching me like this. I could have cried. Then Karen asked me to lie face down, and the urge to cry grew stronger. I rolled over. Now that I had my back to her, and my face was pressed into the hole in the treatment table, I could let out some tears. How long it had been. How long since I'd had skin-to-skin contact. I wanted to embrace her, but she might misunderstand. It wasn't that. My agitation wasn't desire. It had never happened to me before. I'd never liked a woman in that way. It was something else. It was her affection, the force of her youth, the tenderness that her gentle manner awoke in me, the ease with which she moved around the cubicle, her well-defined profile, I don't know, I don't know, but I kept crying in silence, with a mixture of distress, disquiet and joy that I hadn't felt in a long time.

7.

I t was just past eight when she turned out the light and
pulled the cubicle door shut. Once more it was too
late to call Emiliano. Her talks to him were dwindling to
a Sunday ritual. She didn't want to become one of those
Bogotá working mothers whose calls home became
shorter and shorter and more sporadic, whose children
didn't know what to say to them when they did call. Her
initial idea of getting set up and then bringing Emiliano a
few months later hadn't worked out. Those few months
had gone by. Today she had made only 11,000 pesos in
tips. Some days she got 20,000 or more, but other days
she got nothing. It bothered her when she was given a
1,000-peso note. She felt offended; the same hands held
out that amount to beggars on the street.

There weren't many days when she had a string of
clients one after the other. In the idle hours when there
were no clients, almost always the minxes, as Susana
called them, invented all sorts of gossip and flipped
through beauty and celebrity magazines, the same ones
again and again. They commented on celebrity diets, the
accessories this or that actress was wearing during the
TV and Telenovela awards, the love affair a local model

was having with some entrepreneur. Karen also liked looking at the magazines, but she had no time for the malicious remarks some of her colleagues liked to make. She preferred the days when she barely had time to take a breath between clients. The idle hours were when she grew melancholy, wondering where her life was going, as her colleague Deisy read aloud the finer points of the cucumber diet.

When she got home, she would see how much money was under her mattress. She couldn't remember if it was exactly one million, but she knew it was close. She thought once more about bringing Emiliano here with what she'd saved. It would be a risk, but why shouldn't she? The most expensive part would be paying for someone to look after him. Well, that, and having a good roof over their heads, because where she was living wasn't the greatest. Karen fantasised about a neighbourhood where she could let Emiliano stay out late playing with other kids and not need to worry. She had to get a better idea of the cost of things. She had to work out a more accurate budget. She had to get a move on.

Rush hour had come and gone. She didn't have to wait more than ten minutes at the station. Inside the bus, there were no free seats, but she didn't feel like a sardine either. In the mornings, the trip was a misery. People pushed up against each other, which frequently ended in fights. Then there were the wallets, telephones and jewellery that evaporated, and the accidents suffered by those who jumped the rail to dodge the fare, and the stomped feet and bruises that came with travelling some of the public transport routes.

She calculated that in about five stops she would be able to sit down. She was right. By the fourth, after passing Los Héroes shopping centre, Calle 76, Calle 72 and Las Flores park, she nabbed an empty seat by the window. She rested her head against the fogged glass and was lulled by the engine noise. Every now and then she opened her eyes to see where they were. Houses in the area had seen better days. Though Karen didn't know it, the magnificent mansions out the window – now converted into a flea market, brothels and a black market for spare parts – were rich families' weekenders fifty or sixty years before. People scurried like ants, especially around the stations. There were more of them at this time of day, when the details of their faces and bodies disappeared until they were only quick-moving silhouettes. Life would be simpler if she could live around here. Further up from Avenida Caracas, of course, not on top of the mariachi and strip clubs. Close to Marly station, for example, where she could buy Emiliano's school supplies at the large Éxito store when the time came. She would buy him only healthy food – no snack foods, only good things – fruit, yoghurt, string cheese. Things that would nourish him and make him grow up healthy, she thought. She felt a twinge on her backside. The buses were full of fleas. On the coast, there were no fleas, but there were cockroaches. Disgusting fleas.

Nowadays her mother barely responded when Karen asked if Emiliano had a healthy appetite, if he was behaving himself, if she was supervising the time he spent watching TV. 'You just worry about yourself, child,' her mother said, and avoided talking long. She had to turn down the stew, or bring in the washing, or watch her telenovela, or bathe Uncle Juan. There was always something.

If she had money, Karen thought, she would pay for a nurse so her mamá didn't have to clean up after Uncle Juan all the time. He was getting worse. Sometimes he lost control, or forgot, or who knew why, and soiled himself. 'Does it just to annoy me,' her mother said, yet Karen found that hard to believe. She remembered when her uncle used to tell stories all day. His favourite one was about the parrot he loved 'like a daughter'.

He took the parrot everywhere: on his walks to buy lottery tickets, to play dominoes, to have a coffee. It was the longest-lasting, most stable relationship he'd ever known. Or it was until the day someone ran the parrot over.

This was a story with no witnesses, which made it even more doubtful, more sinister. No one saw the parrot get run over. And the strangest thing is, the street in question was a dirt road that cars went down only rarely. It was a neighbourhood of motorbikes, not cars.

One night, when he got home from work at the post office, Uncle Juan and Doña Yolanda sat down to eat.

Karen didn't remember the scene because she was three or four and wouldn't have been at the table. Like every other night, they were eating in near silence. The radio was playing in the background. Uncle Juan liked the soup so much he asked for more. After finishing off the second bowlful, he said to his sister: 'What did you put in this tasty soup?' Not missing a beat, Yolanda answered, 'Sarita the parrot.' Uncle Juan laughed at first, but on seeing how she kept eating, serious, he got up and looked all over the house for his parrot. He didn't find her.

He threw up all night until daybreak, and for several weeks the two didn't speak. When Karen asked her mamá why she did it, she said, 'The parrot was dead, what did you expect me to do, throw it in the bin? Do you think we're rich or something?' Though Karen didn't remember the scene, she did remember asking that question, as well as her mother's reply. Despite her age, Karen knew it was cruel, and that it did irreversible damage to her uncle. From then on, he repeated the story almost daily and, not long after, he became lost in memories of past sporting events and would give a constant running commentary of them, as if his mind could no longer bear being there in that house with them. Her mother's reply was etched in Karen's mind also because it was the first time someone told her they weren't rich. She had never thought about it before, but that didn't make knowing it any less sad.

Yolanda Valdés had no choice but to clean the shit off her brother, spoon-feed him his mash and bathe him like a child. There was no money to put him in an old people's home, or to pay a nurse or a maid. She ended up becoming the maid herself, waiting on her brother hand and foot like a slave in exchange for a place to live and food to eat. And the old man, despite his dementia, every now and then reminded her that the house was his, that it was his money covering their expenses.

Karen knew – her mamá had told her – that her mother's greatest misfortune was giving birth to a girl because 'men do whatever they like, while we women do what falls to us'. Karen was thirteen when she first heard that. From then on, with every woman she knew or met, Karen would ask herself whether she did what she wanted, or what had fallen to her. She also asked herself whether taking care of Uncle Juan fell to her mother or was a cross she chose to bear. She couldn't imagine what her mother would do if she didn't have so many things to complain about. Her mother personified unhappiness, was unhappiness itself.

Since Emiliano was born, Karen had the feeling her mother loved the boy more than she loved her. Perhaps because she saw in him the chance to turn the tide, to change things. Her mother, like her grandmother before her, had the frustration of not having a son to stick up for the Valdés family. But there was something else: her mother was disappointed in her. First for not capitalising on her beauty, and then for getting pregnant by a 'black nobody', as she described Nixon. Yolanda Valdés was a grandmother at thirty-six years of age and felt better prepared to be a mother than when she had Karen at sixteen. No doubt she didn't feel like a grandmother, or at least didn't want to be one.

The bus was now nearing Profamilia, the family planning centre. Someone had told her they performed abortions there, that it was a good clinic, where medical practitioners did everything to the highest standard of hygiene. But wasn't that illegal? Karen asked herself. It was, she answered her own question, but that's where they did them, should she ever need one. Could she be going crazy? Like Uncle Juan? Maybe it was the conversations she caught snippets of throughout the day, on the bus, in the station, in the street, at House of Beauty. Maybe she'd heard one girl say it to another, maybe when they were passing by here, who knew. This area was nice, too. The houses down from the Avenida Caracas and Calle 39 intersection were some of the nicest she'd seen in this city. There were some in the English style, with moss on the walls and little square windows that evoked a warm fire, hot chocolate heated over a low flame, even melted marshmallows. Sadly, most of them were no longer family homes. Now they were businesses, foundations. And people didn't live in them, for safety reasons. In this city, you couldn't have a house with nothing between it and the street. You had to put up obstacles, limits, protective barriers. A guard or two, a fence, preferably electrified, a menacing dog. Only an idiot would leave himself unprotected like that, he'd be fair game. So no one lit the fire in the fireplace behind those little square windows, not any more. What if in Cartagena there'd been a Profamilia and a girlfriend had told her about it? If she hadn't been so silly about Nixon? And if she hadn't had the fear of God ingrained in her? If she'd told someone? Wasn't taking contraceptives almost the same as having an abortion? Weren't they both ways of avoiding a life before it was a life? Why keep a life when no one wants it? She felt embarrassed for thinking this way. It's God who giveth and God who taketh away, no one else, she reminded herself, repeating the phrase she'd heard hundreds of times. Next to her the portly bearded man got off and a young, pregnant woman, sixteen at most and at least seven months along, moved into the space where he'd been. She made as if to sit down but stopped, hovering in the air, her backside about twenty centimetres above the seat. This habit was widespread in Bogotá, Karen had noticed. In fact, whoever didn't let the seat cool after the previous person had left it was considered impolite. Hovering above the seat for seven, ten seconds, the young woman waited for the heat from the bearded man's backside to dissipate. Susana had explained that people did this so as not to be invaded by others' moods.

The young woman sat down. Karen looked at her out of the corner of her eye, but wasn't brave enough to turn towards her. Out of nowhere, she thought about me. She thought about how I was different from her other clients. I seemed like a free woman, at peace with life. She wanted to be like me when she was my age, she told me later. If she were rich, she would like to be rich like me, not like Doña Rosario Trujillo. If she were rich, it wouldn't have mattered that she'd been born a girl, 'because all rich people do well for themselves, men or women. They're not exactly equal, but almost,' she said.

The pregnant young woman bit at a hangnail. Her fingernails were so gnawed down they were almost gone. Her hair was greasy and her expression was fearful. Karen wanted to talk to her, even if just to distract her from whatever was worrying her so much.

'How far along are you?'

'Seven months.'

'So, October, then?'

'Yes, Señora, the beginning of October.'

'And the father's happy?'

'Yes, Señora, he was.'

'He isn't now?'

'Not any more, he's dead.'

The young woman's eyes welled with tears. Karen didn't say anything, but was now looking at her directly, as if she wanted to hypnotise her, or tell her something, but couldn't find the words. The girl moved her fingers towards her mouth again; gently but firmly, Karen took her hand and placed it onto her lap. She left it there, still, her own hand resting on it. That's how they reached the stop on Calle 22, not far from where the street of sin started. On that street prostitutes came in and out of tiled houses like enormous bathrooms, steeped with the smell of detergent, semen, urine and alcohol; nearby was the neon sign for La Piscina, where women stripped and danced under flickering white lights, rubbing their backsides against the jaws of young executives on stag parties until they slipped them a few notes to fondle their nipples.

The streets with the mariachis, where Karen had never set foot, were now behind them. She'd never once been to a bar or club anywhere in this city.

Here there were houses with broken windows; dealers; down-and-outs; transvestites; prostitutes. Many of the prostitutes were old, or fat, or young girls, or sick. But only the wealthy went to La Piscina. Karen had heard that a bottle of whisky cost half a million pesos. Surely the girls were treated well, and didn't let anyone hit them or infect them with one of those disgusting diseases. Her eyelids were drooping with weariness, but since the bus stopped, she craned her neck to see where some girls were going. The pregnant girl had got off and an elderly man was in her place. Karen's stomach grumbled and she tried to remember what she had for lunch. She tried to recall if there was anything to eat at home. She had to go shopping. Maybe on Sunday. It was late now, she just wanted to snuggle under the covers. Her calves, arms, and the tendons in her hands were aching. Only nine stops to go. When the man got off, a woman around the same age as Karen got on. She was attractive, and talked anxiously into her phone. 'But mamá, she's my girl – she's my girl – she's my girl,' she kept saying, like a mantra. Karen closed her eyes. The bus smelled dirty. A mixture of sweat, hair, patchouli, packaged food and cigarettes. Karen wanted to zone out the woman beside her. She wanted to do her calculations. She tried to concentrate. She had started sending her mamá about three hundred pesos each month. It wasn't much. But she had to budget better, it wasn't possible that whole families lived on the minimum wage and she, earning a third more, couldn't make ends meet. Soon after she arrived in Bogotá, her new colleague Maryuri had said: 'You're no good at being poor. You have to make each cent count.' And maybe she was right. Karen felt that she wasn't just bad at being poor, but bad at life in general. Her mamá mocked her, said she thought she was from a better family. It wasn't that. It was that melancholy had holed up inside her since she was small, and she couldn't rid herself of it. Maybe she got that from her papá. She thought she must take after her papá, because she didn't take after her mamá. She'd inherited her mother's sinewy body, long neck, plump lips, and big eyes, but she wasn't outgoing, or loud, or a talker, and she hadn't inherited her love of dance, brandy or rum, either. Her mother often told Karen that she lacked a certain fire. Like when the rice or spaghetti was still a bit hard, 'maybe because you came out of the oven before you were properly done,' said Doña Yolanda, 'maybe that's why you came out bland, like the soul of a mountain person.'

She looked again. They were only at Fucha station. The head of the old man next to her was lolling from one side to the other, like that of a nodding dog. When his head stopped lolling, he found Karen's shoulder particularly comfortable. The cheek! Who does he think he is? she thought, annoyed. She sneezed and soon after they arrived at Restrepo station, where there was always noise and movement. Due to one or the other, the old man woke, made a silly face, rubbed his eyes and, while he didn't say sorry, he did straighten his head and keep it still until Olaya station. She went back to her calculations. She had to check how much money was tucked under her mattress. It was better there than in a bank account. Maybe one of her colleagues could explain the school system and help her find someone to look after Emiliano. The public schools were terrible. Deisy's nine-year-old daughter went to one, and she didn't know how to read or write yet. What a sin, Karen thought. But paying for a private school was another story. She could never afford one.

Perhaps she could bring Emiliano here for Christmas. She'd heard talk of the lights in Parque Nacional. There were some colourful buses that took people to see them. She would have to get a fan for Emiliano, ideally a ceiling fan, like the white one they had at Uncle Juan's that she was sometimes afraid would come flying off and squash them in the middle of the night. Karen remembered her first nights in Bogotá. The cold ground into her bones, and she couldn't sleep; she missed the ceiling fan, its lulling sound, the breeze it made.

It felt like the bus journey would never end. She wanted to get home, count her money, jot down her expenses and the next day do the necessary calculations; she wanted it to be Christmas, to bring Emiliano here, to feel the heat of his little hands, to hold him tight, to sleep curled around him like old times, to wake him with a freshly cooked egg *arepa* and a veal sausage, cultured buttermilk and steamed corn *bollos*. She wanted to see his face when he boarded the Transmilenio bus, when he gazed down on the city from Monserrate. She hadn't been up there yet, but she'd heard it was beautiful.

She looked at her watch; almost nine. Could she have made a mistake? Instead of taking the express she'd hopped on the bus that stops everywhere. No wonder it wasn't packed. Egg *arepa*, she thought with her stomach more than her mind. She had no idea what people saw in the *almojábana* bun. A dry, bland bread that made your tongue claggy. Pale and sweet like the Bogotan people, she thought. Her stomach responded with such a thunderous grumble that the young man beside her raised his eyebrows.

'Would you like some *roscón*?'

'Sorry?'

'I have half a sweet bread in a bag, if you'd like some.'

'Thank you,' she replied, embarrassed.

He had a Valluno accent. He took out the paper bag, opened it carefully and passed it to her. A *roscón* is better than an *almojábana* bun, Karen thought.

'Yes, this week I was able to buy a belt. Not yet, but a colleague lent me two ties. Yes, Señora. Yes, of course. Don't trouble yourself, I was looking at some. Next payday I'll buy my own and give back the one I borrowed,' the young man was saying into his phone.

Karen was so absorbed in the conversation she almost missed her stop. The *roscón* had guava paste inside and she devoured it in two bites. She wondered if Emiliano had ever tried *roscón*. Maybe if he started eating *almojábana* buns as a child, he'd grow up liking them. Having to buy him *almojábana* buns for his breakfast would be funny, she thought, smiling on the inside. He was growing up on fried *arepas*, coconut water and *peto*. How she missed having a fresh *peto* at dusk. It was the perfect rocking-chair drink. Out on the patio, nice and fresh, in a plastic cup. Oh, and tamarind balls, the ones her mother made were always so tasty.

At Uncle Juan's, there were only plastic plates and glasses, and they never bought serviettes. 'What for?' Doña Yolanda said. In the sink was some El Rey soap to get the grease off after each meal. Karen thought maybe that was why her hands were so dry. Here, what woke her wasn't the voice of a seller pushing a *peto* cart, but the loudspeaker from a motorbike loaded with tamales: 'Tamales, tamales, yes, we have tamales, only two thousand pesos, come get your tamales, come through, come through.' Karen would wake up annoyed because it was seven on Sunday morning, the one day people could sleep in, and the street vendors were already out megaphoning their goods. Come through? Karen would wonder, half-asleep. But he's selling from a motorbike. Where could anyone come through to? And she would put the pillow over her head. The bus had already braked when she saw the Santa Lucía stop sign. She jumped off and shot the young man a smile he didn't see.

One of the upsides of living where she did was that it was only three blocks from the station. Apart from a few broken or blown bulbs, the street was well lit. Electricity cables hung down like the entrails of a gutted animal. She walked calmly for the first block, but then she heard police sirens and, after turning down Carrera 19, she came across a commotion next to the Brisas del Sur hostel. About fifteen taxis were blocking the street, and the area had been cordoned off around one of them. On the other side of the street, a body was being lifted into an ambulance. A few bystanders were watching the scene. The taxi drivers were shouting, 'Kill him! Kill him!' and were hurling rocks at a house window while the police tried to contain them. Here in Bogotá, Karen had noticed, people only milled in the streets when there was a death, a terrorist attack, an accident. Anything else, they stayed shut away in their homes. On the coast on the other hand, people put Rimax chairs out in the street, set up their *picó* sound systems, put on a good *vallenato* or *bachata* and raised a nice and cold Costeñita or Águila to their neighbours, whiling away the afternoon.

'What happened?' she asked an old man in pyjamas.

'Someone shot a taxi driver, trying to rob him. Now they want to lynch the thief, he's hiding in that house.'

When she crossed to go down Carrera 20, she saw an armoured riot-control truck approaching. In less than three minutes she was trying to open the door of her building, her pulse speeding and hands shaking. The tear-gas canisters reverberated in her ears. She looked up and thought she saw a light on in her apartment. When she looked down to push open the door, a black cat brushed against her legs. She was watching it go on its way when a press on her shoulder made her turn around. It was a junkie, with sagging jeans and stuck-up hair.

'Neighbour, how are you tonight, other than being as beautiful as a star?' he said with a toothless smile and bad breath.

Karen looked at him a second, gave him a paltry smile and went back to the door knob.

'What's the hurry, princess?' he said, drawing out the final syllable. Karen noticed him glance upwards, just as the light in her apartment turned on and off intermittently.

'What's going on up there?' she said. Her voice trembled. Now she was scared. Then he got out a knife and put it to her throat:

'Nothing we need to report. If you behave yourself, this will have a happy ending for everyone.'

Karen was stunned. Someone was in her apartment, or had just left it. The man held her there, glancing up to the window every few seconds. Karen was too scared to speak. Then there was a noise – was it the building's back door banging shut? – and he gave her a light push and moved away in the shadows. Before he disappeared, she noticed a duffle bag slung over his shoulder, and wondered if her things were in it.

Plucking up her courage, she went inside. On the first floor, there was no sound. The lights were off. The landlord and landlady, who rented out three apartments, lived behind an iron grille with three padlocks. Their dog, Muñeco, was in the central patio. In the first part of the house lived a woman with a girl about ten years old. On the second floor, in the apartment across from Karen's, lived a police officer, his wife and their baby. She went up the stairs as fast as she could, and found the door knob broken, the door open, her clothes on the floor, the mirror cracked in two, the photo of Emiliano thrown on the floor and her statue of the Virgin Mary headless. The TV and radio were gone, as were the gold chain her Uncle Juan had given her as a graduation gift and her Divine Child medal. But she hardly noticed these details because she was only thinking about her bed. She rushed to it. Everything looked in order. The mattress was in place, the bed was made. If it weren't for the mirror, the Virgin and her clothes, she would think nothing had happened. The half-full cup of coffee was in the sink, as she had left it that morning. Breadcrumbs were on the kitchen bench. Her towel was draped on the head of the bed. And yet, on lifting the mattress she discovered that the only thing she couldn't afford to find missing – the only thing that mattered to her, the only thing that made a difference to her life and her son's life, the only thing that justified her living here in this city – was gone.

Karen looked for it all over the apartment, as if it might have switched hiding spots. She searched the bathroom drawer, the saucepans, the drawers of her bedside table, her wardrobe, even the waste basket. She searched the same places again and again, as if her brain had ordered her to repeat the same actions for as long as necessary, anything not to have to accept that the money had gone forever, and there was nothing she could do about it.

8.

His phone rang and Ramelli stretched his leg, accidentally spilling what little whisky was left in the bottle on the parquetry floor. 'Come to my place right away, brother, it's an emergency. We've got a paralytic,' said Diazgranados. He hung up. Getting to his feet, Eduardo kicked the bottle again, then tripped while he tried to pull on a shoe. He was still half drunk. That was when Lucía appeared in the living room to ask where he was off to at that hour.

'A friend's in trouble, he needs my help, I'll tell you about it later.'

Soon after, Lucía would empty the ashtray, clean the house and decide – even jot it down on the calendar in the kitchen – that from that point on, no one would smoke in her house. It was the early hours of 23 July.

They met in the 24-hour Carulla supermarket on Calle 63. Diazgranados was wearing a sky-blue sweater and sunglasses. It was five in the morning. They talked for around seven minutes. It was Ramelli's idea to buy the Tryptanol. He knew in large doses it could cause respiratory arrest. The aim was to avoid a forensic investigation. If they got a credible death certificate, they could get out of an autopsy. They bought the drug. It was Ramelli's job to dress Sabrina appropriately, clean her up, and get a taxi driver they could count on to take her to San Blas Hospital. Once there, they'd have Doctor Venegas, who owed them more than one favour, admit her and write up the certificate. 'Patient with respiratory arrest due to an overdose of tricyclics,' Doctor Venegas would write a couple of hours later. The evidence to corroborate the medical theory: an empty Tryptanol blister in her jacket pocket, and the taxi driver's testimony. And that would be the end of it.

'Venegas's certificate will cost us a couple of million,' Aníbal said to Ramelli while he pushed around a shopping cart loaded with papaya, pineapple, almond milk and a box of cereal.

'Is this really the time for shopping?' Ramelli protested.

'Fucking calm down and look what's in the cart. Take a good look. See any sausages, chorizos, lamb shanks, lard, beans, wine, sherry?'

Ramelli took the cart and looked at his associate again.

'It's a false lead,' he said. 'If whoever's on checkout remembers what I bought, no one will believe it's me.' He burst out laughing.

'You're such a jerk.' Ramelli didn't feel like smiling.

'Come on, give us a smile, brother. And relax a bit while you can because soon you'll be cleaning up and dressing a dead girl.' Aníbal gave him a pat on the back.

'You sound like the godfather,' said Ramelli. 'No, that's not right, that stupid top you're wearing makes you look more like Pablo Escobar.'

'How much is the taxi driver going to cost us?' Diazgranados ignored the insult as he rearranged the shopping.

'Ten,' said Ramelli.

'Sonofabitch! That's what he'd earn in eight or nine months.'

'Any better ideas?'

'No,' lied Diazgranados. 'We'll have to keep an eye on that runt, make sure he doesn't play us. Where did you find him?'

'Relax, he's reliable,' said Ramelli.

They parted ways in front of the chilled meat. Despite his false-lead theory, Diazgranados couldn't help taking a tray of cut-price ribs. Each made his purchase at a different checkout. It didn't occur to Ramelli to wonder why someone who had ties to the paramilitaries, who was responsible for several deaths and had access to the best hitmen around, was putting him in this situation. Until now, Ramelli's own biggest crime was of the strictly white-collar variety: laundering money through a health-care provider to embezzle state funds. And even that was something he did under the influence of his new best friend.

Diazgranados was anxious. The intensification of his paranoia was proportional to his appetite. He was an obese man, yet those who knew him had noticed he'd gone up a size in the past few months. For breakfast he had four eggs, half a kilo of cheese, a jug of juice and three cups of coffee. At eleven, he had his bodyguard fetch him a cheese *arepa*, a chicken empanada, and beef, yuca and guava pastries. When Ramelli confessed to Karen, he said what most astonished him was the way Aníbal ate.

'It frightens me,' he said.

'And it doesn't frighten you that he's a murderer, a criminal?' Karen asked.

'No. It frightens me, sickens me to watch him eat the way he does.'

9.

Karen went to the bathroom, blew her nose, splashed water on her face and called Maryuri to ask if she could stay the night. Maryuri said of course, but not without telling her that their place was very small. Wílmer was on nightshift and almost always got back from work around five in the morning. Karen said it wouldn't be for more than three or four days. She stuffed her clothes into a suitcase. Though she tried to make as little noise as possible, her landlord stopped her on the stair. Then his hand was over her mouth and he was dragging her back to her apartment. Karen tried to shout for help but his hairy hand suffocated her. Karen felt like an idiot. That morning she had seen him on the corner, talking to the young man with the sagging jeans. Why hadn't she realised what was going on? He must have been the one who robbed her. He was going to steal the 400,000-peso deposit he'd charged her when she arrived. And right now he was fondling her breasts through her blouse and biting her neck.

He threw her on the bed and struck her hard, nicking her cheek with the gold stone-encrusted ring that he wore on his right hand. He let go of her mouth to hit her, so Karen shouted. Then his swollen dick was inside her.

Karen stopped shouting, blinking, breathing, didn't understand what was happening, nor even whether it really was happening, until the pain got so bad she couldn't escape it. A choking feeling in her throat stopped her from shouting again or even trying.

Her landlord had always seemed vulgar to her. He was a bore, had filthy fingernails and smelled like rancid cheese. Karen thought she knew when a man wanted her. She hadn't detected anything this time. Until today, the landlord had barely been friendly, seemed indifferent to her presence. Maybe he didn't desire her at all. Maybe he just wanted to destroy her. Or maybe he only wanted to fuck her into submission so she wouldn't make a complaint to the police. Rape as a bureaucratic procedure.

Karen sensed a presence in the room, turned her head. That's when she saw, over her landlord's head, Doña Clara leaning against the doorframe. He must have sensed something, too, because he turned to see his wife watching the scene with a strange expression on her face.

'Oh, hun, the poor girl, what a sin, leave her be already.'

'Fucking pester me just when I'm about to finish!' The landlord pulled out his half-flaccid penis and dressed swiftly.

'Do me a favour and get out of here. You hear me?' he said to Karen, as if what just happened was her fault. 'And if you haven't come down in ten minutes, sweetheart, I'm coming up to get you.'

The woman went over to Karen, who was sobbing in a foetal position, trying to cover herself up.

'Get in the shower and scrub away your shame, you dirty girl,' she said.

Karen obeyed. Despondency overcame her. Even lifting the soap was a momentous task. She should have hated the old woman's complicity with her rapist husband, but she was just grateful to have someone telling her what to do.

'I'm calling you a taxi, you don't want to hail one on the street only to have them take you on a millionaire's ride. When you're having a bad day, the bad luck just keeps on coming.'

Karen had stopped sobbing, but couldn't speak. Her hands trembled. She felt tingles up and down her spine.

The scene would come back to her relentlessly. The notice that read APARTMENT FOR RENT FOR A SINGLE WOMAN had been an invitation to dispossess her, to brutalise her and then send her packing. Karen left her nightlamp behind. The bed and table didn't belong to her, but the lamp had cost her 30,000 pesos and she liked it. Days would go by before the rage flooded her body. For the moment it was only pain, fear, fragility. Enough had happened in one day to fill a lifetime. Not even ten hours had passed since Sabrina Guzmán's funeral.

She didn't tell me what happened until much later, when she was no longer the same woman I'd met that April afternoon in House of Beauty. The landlord's wife gave the taxi driver the address Karen had jotted down on a piece of paper.

'Doña Clara, why?' was all Karen managed to say.

'Well, what are you doing living alone? You have only yourself to blame.' Then she shut the taxi door. Before turning away, she added through the open window: 'For the good of everyone, it would be best if we didn't hear from you again.'

Karen turned to the driver. 'To San Mateo, Soacha, if you would be so kind.'

'Yes, sweetheart. The lady already gave me the address. Lucky it's past eleven, otherwise we wouldn't get there this year.'

Karen leaned her head against the window and let herself be rocked by the car movements. Chico Trujillo was singing on the radio about kisses and caramel and heaven, and with each stanza she felt her stomach turning.

'Señor, could you stop a moment.'

'Of course,' said the taxi driver, pulling over.

Karen opened the door and threw up in the gutter. The taxi driver handed her a cloth and asked:

'Am I going too fast?'

'No, it's not that,' said Karen and closed her eyes. 'Let's go, please.'

IO.

Sometimes Karen appears in my dreams. Her dark skin, straight hair and straight nose. Her presence stirs a restlessness in me that I put down to her youth. To her beauty. I don't want, can't bear to acknowledge anything greater, anything resembling desire, carnal appetite. Perhaps because I've never felt anything like it, perhaps because even if I had felt it, I wouldn't have recognised it, trained as I've always been to love men. Karen was so natural. In a place where not even flowers grow in the ground, it was almost an affront. I'm not even sure if that unsuspecting young woman is truly the reason for my disquiet, for what we might call my desire. I'm not sure it can be explained away as having to do with the fact that I'm ageing. After all, we're always ageing, ever since the day we're brought into this world. Yet it takes us so long to grow aware of it. We are blind to so much. We don't see ourselves fade.

As I enter House of Beauty, I notice my hair is smelling foul, so I decide to have it hennaed. 'Burgundy,' I say to Nubia.

Little by little, I get used to being assailed by memories. They are crisp, ravenous, indifferent to my recent history. My mother powdering me in the boudoir in our island house; a lover kissing me on the beach beneath the full moon; sitting on my father's knee, smelling the Jean Marie Farina lotion on his newly shaved, strong jaw; Aline's birth; her first day of school; my naked body after a tireless lovemaking session. My body, not what it used to be, now has me lost, orphaned from myself. Though I'm healthy, as Lucía would say – she has that enviable gift of always focusing on the good. Yet I don't think of myself as healthy. I feel unwell, or at least absent, gone, forsaken, replaced by another I don't know, nor want to get to know, in my constant nostalgia for the woman who's gone. Where have you gone? I try, but these ideas of a suffering woman, a woman who allows herself to be flooded by nostalgic longing, leave me as soon as I hear the water start to run. I submit to Nubia's hands in my hair.

House of Beauty takes me in. I'm submerged in the silence and the expensive perfumes, the rosewater, oils and shampoo. I want to stay here, I tell myself, while I think of an excuse for yet another massage, another wax, though it hasn't been long enough for that. Another hair colour – that's it, another colour. Nubia is shampooing my hair so gently, almost affectionately. She's stroking my scalp while I invent a memory of my mother washing my hair with chamomile shampoo, humming a song in French.

'She's become one of our best clients,' says Annie, her cherry lips even more voluptuous, more tempting. She smiles. She has fake eyelashes, I note, and what months ago seemed vulgar now seems lovely. Provocative. I smile back. I don't want to leave this land of women with dainty manners. I want to stay here forever.

'Would you like to hear about our passport?' Annie says in a soft voice while her lovely hands move with finesse.

'A passport?'

'We offer it to our best clients. It includes therapies for skin, body and hair, as well as relaxation, hydration, cleansing and rejuvenating treatments, among others. Bearing in mind that you come two or three times a week, you might find it great value. For women like you, House of Beauty is a home away from home, and we want to you feel completely at ease here. Would you be interested in taking the package?'

II.

Three weeks after her daughter had been buried, Conseulo Parades woke in a cold sweat. In her dream, Sabrina had been crying inconsolably, her body bruised.

When her breathing returned to normal, she dialled her ex-husband's number. She didn't care that it was three in the morning. On the other end, Jorge Guzmán's phone went to voicemail. Since his daughter's death, he didn't give a damn about anything. His second wife had been understanding for almost a month, but now she was furious. Her husband had neglected his business, and barely said a word to her, or to their five-year-old daughter.

When the telephone rang a second time, she was the one who woke. Jorge was snoring thunderously, still wearing his clothes and shoes. She had fallen asleep before hearing him arrive around midnight.

'Hun, your phone,' she said, giving him a shove.

Impatient, she squeezed his nose between finger and thumb. Jorge opened his eyes and sat up in bed. His wife put his phone to his ear.

'Jorge, is that you?'

'What happened? What time is it?'

On the other end, Consuelo had started crying again.

'It's Sabrina. I had a dream. Our little girl was crying, she was battered, Jorge, and crying.'

'A dream?' said Jorge, his voice bleak.

'Promise me one thing, just one,' said Consuelo between sobs.

'What?'

'Come with me tomorrow morning to the Prosecutor's Office. Do you really believe our girl would commit suicide? They didn't even do an autopsy, so how could they know that … Where did they take her? Where was she that night? I want to know the truth.'

'What did Sabrina say?' asked Jorge.

'When?'

'In the dream, Consuelo, where else.'

'She said, "I didn't want to die, Mamá, I didn't want to, forgive me for leaving, forgive me …"'

'Did you talk to the beautician?'

'I did. She didn't tell me anything, but she must know something. Well, she did tell me something, she asked me why we hadn't insisted on an autopsy.'

After a long silence, Jorge spoke: 'I'll pick you up at eight.'

12.

You can learn almost anything from a textbook. But when you have limited street smarts and little or no experience with actual cases, classic indicators could be staring you in the face and you wouldn't see them. Or want to see them. I now know that Karen wasn't the same after the night she left her apartment in a taxi that took her from Santa Lucía to San Mateo, her entire life packed into a suitcase.

Two minutes or fewer are enough to change everything. I should have connected the dots. On my second appointment with Karen after the minister's daughter's wedding, I noticed she was absent, distracted. She spread oil on me twice and then opened and closed the cubicle door, took the cubicle phone off the hook and hung it up again. For a second I thought she was doing it deliberately to make me laugh, a little Chaplin skit. But then I noticed the deep rings under her eyes, her dull gaze, her thinness.

'Are you eating?' I asked.

'More or less.'

Now she had a static smile in place, like a jester's, a smile that didn't match the rest of her expression, much less whatever she was thinking.

'And are you sleeping okay?'

'What does that matter, Doña Claire?'

I'd irritated her. Then I noticed that her make-up was more pronounced. Her lips were cherry red, like the receptionist's. Her eyeliner was very dark, and she was wearing blusher and mascara.

'I haven't been myself lately,' she mumbled.

And at that moment I noticed a cut on her arm, like the wounds I've known some patients to self-inflict after traumatic events.

'What's the matter, Karen?'

'Forget it … What's a woman my age doing living alone, that's asking for trouble.'

'What are you talking about?'

'A situation I had with my landlord. He made me, but all the same I shouldn't wear such tight clothing.' She went quiet. 'And there's no good reason for a woman to live alone. I have only myself to blame,' she added, as if reciting a lesson.

'I don't know what happened, Karen, but whatever it was, you can't blame yourself,' I said.

'Sometimes I find it hard to breathe, Doña Claire. I keep getting palpitations, like my body's out of control, and sometimes it's as if someone's squeezing the air out of me …'

'I can write you a prescription for a tranquilliser. But tell me, did something serious happen?'

'I don't need a psychologist,' she replied curtly.

'What about a friend?'

'We're not friends,' she said. 'I shouldn't have run my mouth off. Shall I get your bill ready?'

I took her hand and noticed her dry skin. I turned it over, looking at it.

'Now you're going to check to see I'm clean, like Doña Josefina does?' she said as she moved away.

'It's not that. Your skin's very dry.'

'I have to wash my hands all the time, the dirt won't come off.'

'Karen, you need to seek help.'

'With all due respect, Doña Claire, the only thing I need is to bring Emiliano here from Cartagena and to get on with my life.'

'That sounds good, I think you're right,' I said.

'You say that because you don't know what's going on.'

'I don't know because you haven't told me. But I trust you. I think you're a good woman and will do the right thing.'

'You're talking to me as if I'm slow,' said Karen brusquely. 'Just because you're a doctor doesn't make me stupid.'

Her hostility was completely out of character. It was as if something, or someone, had abducted the real Karen and left someone else in her place.

'Nothing will ever be the same again.' She let out a sob, but quickly contained herself. 'If only I could sleep,' she added.

'I can give you something to help with that.'

Karen didn't respond, but watched me as if awaiting my next move. I dug into my handbag in the hope I would find what I was looking for. And there it was, a box of Zolpidem. I trained in psychiatry before specialising in therapy, and I still receive visits from drugs reps.

'This is sleeping medication, take one pill every night.'

Karen tucked it into her uniform pocket and left to write up my bill.

Downstairs at reception, while I was paying Karen approached me and said:

'All the time these images keep replaying in my head … Can the pills take them away?'

'That might need therapy.'

'I don't have the time, or the money.'

'I can help you,' I insisted.

'I just want to get the film reel out of my head.'

'And what happens? In the film, what happens?'

Karen went quiet. Her dull gaze went far away again.

'Maybe with God's help,' she said, and went quiet.

'You know you can talk to me,' I said. I paid the bill and left.

Weeks later the jigsaw pieces started falling into place. Victims of sexual abuse tend to be hyperalert to any stimuli that bring back what happened. They display evasiveness, defensiveness or emotional numbness, a lack of motivation, and they are often suicidal. The idea of going home alone in the dark filled Karen with terror. Because of this, at night she preferred company – spending it on the street, or in someone's arms – so as not to have to face the dark alone.

13.

B ut it wasn't just that Luis Armando reeked of alcohol. It was the dim room, the cocaine spread on the table, the guttural sound he made every few seconds as if he wanted to swallow a toad, the furious way he shook his head, the way he licked his lips time and again, the clicking sound as he worked his jaw, the clumsy way he scratched his nose until it went red. He even drew blood, yet never lost his smile.

He greeted her with a rough kiss that made her mouth bleed. Sabrina wanted to tell him, wanted to say he'd hurt her and she didn't like it, but she remembered her mother's words – 'If you don't have something nice to say, don't say anything at all' – so she kept quiet and let him do what he wanted: she let him pour her a glass of whisky and force her to drink it; let him take a line of cocaine and rub it on her gums, clumsily sticking his fingers in her mouth; let him tear off her white school shirt; let him rummage around in the satchel she'd brought, looking for who knows what; let him spread her clothes around the room.

Now Sabrina thought she'd made a mistake, but the time for thinking had passed. Her mind was numb. Her body barely responded. She felt weak; she was scared. Nevertheless, her habit of obeying, of pleasing, of never offending, prevented her from moving. That – or else the fear, or the pain, or the sadness – kept her as still as a statue in the half-light. Still, except for her heart, which felt about to explode. The man before her was her Prince Charming, or so she'd managed to convince herself. She'd pieced together his personality from the impressions she'd got from two or three outings and a few calls. He was the son of a politician, he'd said he loved her. She wasn't going to run out like a little girl just because her lip was bleeding, just because there was a little coke on the table. She was so naive; she'd imagined romantic music in the background, a bottle of champagne and some balloons or roses, or both of those things, on the bed and floating in the room, which in her imagination had smelled of anything but drunkenness. But her mother had told her, 'Matrimony is a cross to bear.' It's not easy, she'd said, it's not simple, love is not simple. What had she thought, that everything would be a Disney film, that everything would be roses and little love hearts? No, just because he didn't stroke her face like he had on other occasions, just because he was a little drunk, she wasn't about to go running away like a little girl. She wasn't a little girl any more, never would be again.

14.

The autopsy performed on Sabrina Guzmán Paredes found high doses of cocaine in her body, which would suggest death by overdose. Signs of small haemorrhages (petechiae) were found in the conjunctiva of the eye. There were intramuscular haematomas on the neck and petechiae on the thorax, which, according to experts, are typically signs of a death by asphyxiation. They were not conclusive in this case because of the body's decomposition.

The toxicological report stated that on Sabrina Guzmán Paredes's body cocaine was found in a quantity of two parts per million, as was benzoylecgonine. It explained that these doses were very high, given that, on the body of a regular user, levels of 0.1 to 0.5 parts per million were usually present. Above one part per million, convulsions can be present, among other effects.

While the report gave respiratory arrest caused by cocaine intoxication as a possible cause of death, the likelihood that the death was due to physical violence remained open.

Nevertheless, because more than ten days had passed and the body had been exhumed, it was not possible to establish the causes of the bruising and petechiae present on the body. Thus, it was impossible to establish whether it was rape or consensual sexual relations, and whether the bruising was due to physical violence or an accident. Traces of semen were detected on the body of the victim.

Finally, the expert opinion of forensic medicine ruled out the possibility that Sabrina Guzmán Paredes was a regular cocaine user, because there were none of the usual indications of frequent consumption. Nor were there traces of amitriptyline in the body that would corroborate the use of Tryptanol as the cause of death.

The state of the body meant it was not possible to determine if there were skin abrasions.

The pathologist concluded that establishing the cause of death was at the discretion of the relevant authorities, once they clarified the remaining evidence uncovered over the course of their investigation. The case was passed into the hands of the Prosecutor's Office. Signed on the third of August.

15.

The San Agustín church is one of the few relics from the seventeenth century still standing in the capital. I got out a few blocks before it because of the parade of SUVs, bodyguards and police. Out of the seven hundred guests, I must have been the only one who came in a taxi.

I wanted to flee, but it was too late. The Gregorian chants coming from the church drew me in. I quickened my pace and looked away when I encountered the sore-covered leg of a destitute man. The next was more difficult to avoid because he was right in front of me. He was old, stank of urine, and was crying, his hand outstretched. I racked my brain for the last time I'd been in the city centre and came up with nothing.

On the invitation, there was no mention that the Catholic wedding would be celebrated with the old Latin rites. I sat down where I could, right in time to see the bride enter on the arm of the minister. She was wearing a magnificent gown, a beaded sweep of white that glided across the red carpet from the dark street to the heavenly altar. Everything was strange, yet it was impossible not to feel awed by the scent of jasmine, lilies and chrysanthemums, by the delicacy of the orchids, the thousands of white candles, the opening notes of a Handel Suite.

Special permission had been sought from the Colombian Episcopal Conference to have the rite carried out in Latin, the priest with his back turned to the faithful. I would discover this the next day, on opening the newspaper and seeing photos of the wedding and a detailed account of what happened at the reception. Yet I didn't need to read the paper to understand that a two-hour ceremony as traditional as this was a clear statement, especially coming from a minister who professed belief in the Virgin, who dedicated all his efforts to abolishing abortion under any circumstance, and who opposed homosexuality as if it were heresy. I would also read that the seventeenth-century ornaments and chalices were lent by the bishop himself as a token of his esteem for the bride and groom.

Wherever I looked, there was a minister, a judge, a politician. Amid the plethora of power, I searched for a familiar face. I didn't find one.

I twitched when the cardinal read out a personal message from the Pope for the bride and groom. And when he criticised same-sex marriage in front of the entire political power of a nation that is nominally secular, I bristled.

The priest said 'the treacherous Jews' soon before Mozart's *Coronation Mass* sounded. But wasn't Mozart a Protestant? I said to myself. I closed my eyes and breathed deep the smell of jasmine. I didn't want to be there. If I listened, I felt troubled, but if I limited myself to enjoying the scene and to letting the music, the smell of flowers, the magnificence of the church and the beauty of the candelabras wash over me, then I felt overcome by an ecstatic, airy stillness.

My hands were sweating, and I felt a despondency that neither Schubert's 'Ave Maria' nor 'Gloria in Excelsis' alleviated.

The God I didn't believe in must have had mercy on me because, despite my fears, the Mass concluded without anyone being struck down. The bride was filing down the aisle as people threw rose petals from the first pews. I would have to wait for the others to leave before I could. Amid the commotion, I saw Lucía Estrada's face. It was as though all this time I'd been shipwrecked and now had found some driftwood to cling to. I made my way through the crowd to catch up to her and, in the doorway of the church, grabbed her by the arm:

'Lucía!'

'Claire, my dear!' she said, turning around with a smile. 'I didn't expect to see you here!'

'Likewise!'

'Isn't it awful?' Lucía murmured.

'I thought I was going to die.'

'Well, we survived,' she said.

Ramelli was further ahead, alongside Aníbal Diazgranados, his wife and one of his sons. He waved a hand to indicate that Lucía should hurry up.

'Want to come with us?' Lucía asked.

'I don't know, I don't really feel like going to the reception.'

'We can drop you off on the way, then. You don't have your car?'

'That would be fabulous, I don't like the idea of being out on the street at this hour. Sure there's room?' I asked when I saw Ramelli and Diazgranados getting in.

'There's plenty,' insisted Lucía.

After so much effort, I decided I may as well go by the reception to greet the bride's parents at least. In the first SUV were Diazgranados's driver, his wife, his son and Lucía.

'If it's okay with you, you can hop in the one behind,' said Lucía.

I couldn't help glancing inside. I wanted to see what the son of one of the most questionable and powerful politicians in the country looked like. I smiled, and he smiled back. In contrast to his father, he had fine features, a square jaw and long legs.

I wanted to know his name, but it seemed a little forward to ask now, when everyone was waiting for me. I hurried to the second SUV and got in. Eduardo was in the passenger seat. Beside me in the backseat was Aníbal Diazgranados. I'd never been so close to him before. His face was familiar because I'd seen him on the news, but I'd never felt his breath on me, or had him ogle my décolletage.

'Ramelli my brother, stop being rude, tell me who this voluptuous autumnal beauty is.'

Ramelli turned around to see me cornered against the window, absorbed in the street, while Aníbal's eyes were all over me. He had what seemed like an ironic smile on his face.

'Minister, meet Claire Dalvard, a well-regarded psycho-analyst. She studied at the Sorbonne.'

'Fuck, you're kidding, a goddamn doctor!'

'Claire. Pleased to meet you.' I held out my hand, then was disgusted by the way he took it between both of his and kissed it with affection. 'Of course, I've heard about you.'

'Whatever you've been told, it's all lies,' said Aníbal. 'Tell me something, gorgeous, what does an hour with you cost?'

'I can give you my consulting-room phone number. I should have a business card in here some-where.'

'Please, humour me with a *vallenato*, it's like a funeral in here,' he said to the driver as he tucked my card into his pocket.

'Of course, Minister.'

'My little Luis loves this song,' said Diazgranados between shouting the chorus.

When we were turning from Avenida Calle 100 onto Carrera 7 he leaned across my legs to get out a silver flask that was under the passenger seat.

'Have a drink, my brother,' he said to Ramelli, who accepted obediently.

'Doctor?'

'No, thank you. Can I ask you something?'

'Of course, Doctor,' said Diazgranados.

'Do you have a son called Luis Armando? Who works for an oil company?'

'I sure do. How do you know?'

'Through my daughter Aline; she works with him,' I lied.

I went back to looking out the window. We were arriving.

'Brother, so are we going to Sincelejo on Monday?' Aníbal asked Ramelli, as if he hadn't attributed any importance to my question.

'Sure, I'm coming along,' said Ramelli.

Aníbal turned to me. 'This guy sitting here, the Master, he isn't just wise – he's turned out to be a good business-man, too.'

'Oh, really?'

'Tell Claire about your business dealings in health.' Aníbal took another swig.

Ramelli looked put out.

'Well, we're based mainly on the coast. We don't have much of a presence in Bogotá.'

'But what part of the health sector do you run?' I asked.

'We've got the San Blas Hospital licence.'

'I don't know how you find the time for so much,' I said.

'Me neither,' Ramelli said while Aníbal sang along to a Jorge Oñate song.

'Looks like we're here, finally. Are you going to wish me a happy birthday?' Diazgranados asked.

'It's today?'

'Sure is, the fourteenth of August. I'm a Leo. The power sign. And aside from that I'm very passionate,' he added in a softer voice.

'I don't believe in star signs,' I said.

I opened my handbag to check my reflection in my compact and touch up my lips.

'You're heavenly like that,' Aníbal said. He was starting to wear me out.

He shook the flask over his mouth to get at the last drops of whisky. Meanwhile, the parade of SUVs and security convoys at the entrance of the Country Club was starting to block traffic. I couldn't see my chance to get away. Maybe I could have a drink with Lucía, I thought naively, not foreseeing how much longer it would take for us to get into the room where the reception was taking place.

'The last drop?' offered Diazgranados. 'It's on Health Cross. Isn't that right, Ramelli?' he added with a loud laugh.

'Who would have thought that health was such good business?' I said sarcastically.

'Oh, Doctor, please. Don't try to tell me you haven't worked that out,' said Diazgranados.

As soon as I could, I got out – almost jumped out – of the SUV. A blue carpet and white marquee walkway mimicked a tunnel. The guests made their way along it from the valet parking.

The night was clear, with a full moon. Photographers followed the recently arrived guests, firing their cameras. For the VIPs, there was a platform with professional lights where they were asked to pose for the 'bride and groom's album'. Brushing against one side of the marquee walkway, trying to pass by unseen, I went as far ahead as possible, avoiding the photographers. There was a small group around Minister Obando, the minister for internal affairs, and his wife, Teresa.

'Claire! Thank you for coming!' said Teresa.

We hugged amid flashes and glances.

'Everything has turned out beautifully.'

'Thank you, yes, our girl is very religious, we wanted her to be happy.'

The minister came over to greet me.

'So, you're the famed Claire.'

'You're the famous one, Minister.'

'We've been trying to find time to reschedule that appointment, but haven't been able to,' he said.

The plural surprised me.

'You're both coming? I don't usually do couples therapy.'

'My wife's concerns are my own, so if she wants to talk to a therapist, I have no choice but to support her by tagging along.'

I looked at my school friend. She smiled, her gaze dull. I noticed the gold, diamond-encrusted crucifix that hung from her neck and took two steps to the side to let the guests behind me greet the couple. I wanted to say goodbye to Lucía, but I'd lost her among all the people. I turned and walked towards the Country Club entrance, where they found me a driver to take me home. I was about to leave when I bumped into Diazgranados's wife, Rosario Trujillo.

'Do we know each other?' I said.

'Yes,' she said. 'House of Beauty, I often go there. If I'm not mistaken, we see the same girl.'

'Karen?' I asked.

'Of course,' she said, before excusing herself and moving towards her husband.

16.

It was past three in the morning. The venue was almost
empty. There were a drunk person or two, a woman
who looked like a model playing with the microphone on
stage, Jorge Celedón's band packing up their instruments
and Diazgranados tossing back the dregs of the drinks
still on the table. Claire hadn't set foot in the reception
and Lucía had gone who knows where, with who knows
whom.

That night, Eduardo was lonely. It seemed that every
man around him was dancing with the love of his life,
just when he was starting to accept that Lucía had
stopped loving him. He didn't want to go home alone,
switch the TV to a porn channel and masturbate until
he fell asleep. He decided to call Gloria, but she didn't
answer. He had to book her in advance, especially if it
was a weekend. Then he remembered she'd given him
the agency number. He searched his wallet for the card
and called. He collected his suit jacket, and left in search
of his SUV.

Karen slipped on black lace underwear, a satin sleeveless
blouse and high heels.

She put on cherry lipstick and painted her eyes an intense black. Susana picked out her clothes, and gave her tips for her first date as an escort. Everything had happened so fast. Susana had answered her questions, and then suggested she go with a few of Susana's clients first, to see how she felt about it. In exchange, Karen would give her a commission. If she felt comfortable, Susana would introduce her to the agency formally, so she could be put in the catalogue. If all went well, she could build up a pool of clients and, later, work independently. The numbers were tempting. Plus, her friend explained, doing it for just a few years would make her enough to buy a house. At the end of the day, she had nothing to lose by trying it out. The agency called Susana to tell her a client was looking for Gloria. Since she wasn't available, could Susana go? The circumstances were perfect. With two, at most three, clients, Karen could recover the money she had saved in eight months.

The New Hope buildings are wider than they are tall. They rise in a half-moon around a false meadow, the centrepiece of which is a jet of water, as artificial as the grass, falling on grey pebbles. The effect of the building's blue windows, and the sound of a waterfall in the middle of what looks like a golf green, means anyone used to buildings in Bogotá's distinctive redbrick is dumbfounded when they come across this alien construction on the Avenida Circunvalar. Karen found it beautiful.

'Remind me of your name?' the doorman said.

'Pocahontas.'

'Pocahontas what?'

'Just Pocahontas.'

The doorman shot her an incredulous look. He was wearing a headset and a royal-blue uniform that set him apart from any other doorman she had seen before.

'I'm sorry, Señora, but I need to see your ID. Management rules.'

Karen went red. She felt like an idiot. Pocahontas, she said to herself as she opened her wallet and passed him her card. He looked at her, looked at the card, and jotted the information down, as well as the time of arrival.

Following the instructions, she went out to a Japanese garden lit by a soft, bluish light.

She took off her heels, to make as little noise as possible when crossing the wooden platform that stretched across the garden from one building to the other. At the entrance was an extensive lobby with oversized furniture and marble sculptures. This time a woman in a black uniform asked for her ID, and once more jotted down the time of arrival before requesting the lift through a digital monitor. She'd been so stupid saying Pocahontas, such a child. She kept kicking herself.

Feeling completely out of place, she got into the middle lift and closed her eyes. She opened them again and saw the Japanese garden, the city further below it. She was nervous, and tried to contain the tremor in her hands. The lift stopped, the doors opened and on the other side she found Eduardo Ramelli. He was wearing a white bathrobe. He was barefoot. He smiled warmly and, for a second, Karen was less afraid. In any case, she was surprised. On the one hand, she was disappointed to discover that the Master solicited these kinds of services; on the other, she was relieved he was her client because she supposed he wouldn't harm her. She tried to smile as she went into the apartment, forcing herself to act naturally.

'A drink?' he asked, as he took her jacket.

'Yes, please,' she said, realising that he hadn't recognised her.

Ramelli poured an amber liquid into a wide cup, and she drank it in long gulps.

'You're new to this?'

'Yes, Señor,' she said, putting the empty glass on the table.

'Drop the "Señor". Have we met?'

'I don't think so,' Karen lied.

They were in a living room with white furniture. Karen didn't want to sit down in case she dirtied something. In any case, Eduardo didn't ask her to sit. He did ask her to take a shower before going through to the bedroom, and handed her an unopened antibacterial soap. Then he showed her a robe and disposable slippers, for when she got out of the shower.

In the bedroom, everything was white. The king-sized bed looked onto a marble chimney recessed in the wall.

To the west, a view of Bogotá could be seen through a large window that stretched from floor to ceiling.

The cognac had worked its effect on her. Her head was spinning and she felt mildly numbed. At first, he touched her, but then it was her turn. In the beginning, she felt a little disgust. The sensation in her mouth was unpleasant, especially when she had to swallow saliva and make sure not to gag. But her client was kind and in less than an hour she was in another taxi going back to Susana's.

'You have a rare beauty. I'd like to see you again,' Ramelli had told her, counting out the money at the door.

'Call me,' said Karen. She could be informal now that she was more relaxed. She took the money and tucked it into her handbag.

'Where to, Señorita?' the taxi driver asked. According to the identity card on display, his name was Floriberto Calvo. Calle 60 and Carrera 10, said Karen, overcome by relief that she didn't have to say San Mateo, Soacha, Santa Lucía, or Corintio.

The radio was tuned to La Cariñosa station, and the news programme *Warning Bogotá* was on. The unmistakable voice boomed into the Chevrolet Spark:

Warning, Bogotá! Unbelievable! Thinking he was being cheated on, a construction worker stabbed his wife twenty times in the Bosa area.

Extra, Extra! A drunk set a sergeant on fire in Kennedy after he tried to shut down a game of Tejo.

Unbelievable! A reveller in Bogotá's south-west killed a bouncer for denying him entry.

Karen tried to sleep, but with those news items it was impossible.

'Excuse me, could we listen to something else?'

'Of course, sweetheart.' Floriberto searched for another channel.

Karen liked the *Warning* voice. On the coast, she listened to the programme a lot, but tonight she didn't feel like hearing about people killing each other. She had a headache.

Most of the babies that died at birth in health centres on the Atlantic Coast last year had active records at the health-care provider Caprecom. Irregularities were found in close to twenty healthcare providers in several regions. The comptroller is making headway on a report that will be made public by the middle of next month. It is estimated that, to date, the health-sector fraud amounts to three billion pesos. The comptroller found inconsistencies in the management of health resources for the poorest in more than one hundred munici-palities across the country. In Cartagena alone, more than ten deceased persons have active records, not to mention the more than 3,000 cloned patients' records …

Karen fell asleep, so she didn't hear Health Cross mentioned among the healthcare providers being investigated. In any case, she wouldn't have made the connection with Ramelli, much less with the 600,000 pesos she had tucked into her handbag.

After leaving the Santa Lucía apartment, Karen had stayed at Maryuri's in San Mateo for one night, sleeping on a mat. She had arrived at midnight, while Wílmer was working and the little girl sleeping. Maryuri was too tired to listen to her. They lived in an area covered in dust, where they could afford a 45-square-metre apartment in an enclosed complex with a pool, a communal area and a park for the little ones. Grilles covered all the windows and broken glass was cemented into the rooftops. Maryuri had been married two years. Her little girl would turn one soon, and Karen was invited to the party.

Maryuri gave her friend a sleeping mat to set up in the middle of the living area, where a fridge also stood. The kitchen was barely a bench with a stovetop and a miniature sink. Karen lay down on the floor, which smelled of rotten fruit. She had broken, jittery dreams. Twice she got up to vomit. She heard Wílmer arrive in the early hours of the morning. She sensed him come over to her and draw away the quilt to see who she was. She closed her eyes, faked relaxed breathing. She remembered his square jaw, broad shoulders, thick hair, olive skin and large, green eyes with long eyelashes and a skittish look.

When he was close, Karen smelled cigarettes, sweat, rain and gasoline. She wanted to hug him but contained herself. Of course, he thought she was sleeping.

An hour later the alarm sounded. This was followed by Maryuri's steps, cries, the smell of coffee, the little girl's exclamations as her mamá fed her an egg. Karen felt as if everything was happening somewhere above her. Those morning smells and family sounds comforted her a moment, until she remembered. A huge melancholy swept over her again. Maryuri stroked her hair and gave her a kiss on the forehead after putting the dishes in the sink:

'You've got rings under your eyes, sleep a bit longer. I'm taking the little one to kindergarten and then I'm off to work. I'll tell Willy to give you a lift.'

17.

He only took her to House of Beauty because Maryuri asked him to. Karen peered out the window, thinking that the city looked uglier than ever. There were other taxis in the parking lot.

'Call my phone,' Wilmer said.

Karen obeyed. She got out her phone and dialled the number Wilmer dictated to her. She heard it ring.

'Now save my number. And I'll have yours, too,' he said, his tone authoritarian.

'What do you need my number for?' Karen asked.

'What do you think?' he said. He looked her up and down and didn't add anything. Karen hoped he would call. When they arrived she realised he'd put the taximeter on.

'Now you know, you owe me 36,000 pesos,' was the last thing he said.

Karen got out of the taxi thinking she would have to find somewhere else to stay so she could leave San Mateo that night. As soon as she arrived, she shut herself in the lavatory. She took out a razor blade and made a minuscule cut on her heel. She tried it out a few times on one foot, then on the other. Then she threw up, though she'd had barely half an *arepa* for breakfast. She put on her uniform and went into her cubicle.

That day, at around three, the cubicle phone sounded. It was Susana asking Karen if she was free:

'I can come up and we could have lunch together? I've got ten minutes.'

And that's how it went. She arrived with a pear and a mortadella sandwich; she gave half to Karen, who got some potato chips out of her bag and, right there in the cubicle, they improvised a picnic.

'You look down, Karen.'

'I'm between homes at the moment and was wondering, I don't know if it's too much to ask ...'

'Want to stay at mine for a few days?'

'Are you sure?'

'Positive. We can trial it a few days to see how we go. My place is small but it's well located, it's in the north.'

For Karen, 'it's in the north' were the magic words. It didn't matter that sometimes Susana seemed coarse to Karen, a bit vulgar; she spoke loudly, wore tight clothing and held her gaze in a way that was sometimes intimidating. For the time being, she had no better option.

When they finished work, Karen and Susana left together. Her new friend took a taxi, as if it was something you did every day. Karen kept quiet. For a while now she'd noticed that Susana had a lot more money than she could earn at House of Beauty.

Susana's apartment was in an exclusive area. It was small and there were only a few pieces of furniture, all of them modern and good quality. As soon as they arrived, Susana took a bottle of white wine out of the fridge and poured Karen a glass. The surprises kept coming. It was like being on the set of a telenovela. The two shiny red chairs, the Andy Warhol poster, the sequined curtains: everything seemed sophisticated and at the same time strange.

Four nights later, Karen would go to New Hope for her first escort service. Later, during one of our talks, we concluded that in the early hours of the same morning, when she was getting into bed after spending the night with Ramelli, I was getting up in my Calle 93 apartment, fifty blocks distant, in the same russet dawn.

I find it curious that no one mentions the singular beauty of the light in this city. If I were an artist I would get up at dawn and try to capture that glazed terracotta coming down the mountain. I would have liked to be an artist. Maybe a photographer. I'd do a project taking photos of all different people at precisely the same time. For example, at 4.57 a.m. The lens would capture a mature woman sitting up in bed, wearing a silk nightgown, her face pale and wrinkled; on the bedside table a silver glass, the water still cold, and Emma Reyes's book; and, spread out behind her, a view of the city. In another image would be Karen, in a taxi counting her money, her make-up smudged and her expression tense.

On my way to the kitchen, I picked up the newspaper. I prepared an orange juice while the coffee machine did its thing. I went back to bed with a tray of toast, juice and coffee. I lay back with the newspaper and noticed a faint headache. Just two whiskies before the wedding. I shook my head. Ageing takes its toll. I took two sips of juice, adjusted my glasses and balanced the newspaper in one hand and the coffee in the other. Like many women my age, I have well-developed fine motor skills, thanks to the lessons taken for typewriting, embroidery, crochet and the like.

I scrutinised a special feature about the health-sector fraud. I almost spilt my coffee when I saw Health Cross and, following it, Ramelli named as legal representative. The report explained how healthcare providers invent patients and clone their records, and keep deceased patients active in the system, so they can pocket government reimbursements. I remember our conversation on the day of the wedding. I'd heard Diazgranados was a complete and utter scoundrel. His face is in the newspapers and on the evening news almost every other week, but nothing ever comes of it. The name Aníbal Diazgranados didn't appear anywhere. As for Ramelli, I was intrigued to know how Lucía could have spent thirty years by his side.

In the social pages, I came across photos of the wedding. Accompanying them was a gossip piece written by a young woman fascinated by the excesses of what she termed 'a wedding of old'. Fed up with reading, I turned to the opinion columns. Often, I don't recognise the names of the writers. I'm not sure if they're getting younger, if those I know are slowly filling the obituary pages, or if I've lost touch. Perhaps a little of all three.

The unhappiness I felt at the wedding reminded me of my fifteenth birthday party. Determined to do it Colombian style, Papá bought me a silk dress and let me have champagne, and we danced the waltz. I had to accept the bouquets different boys gave me. Now I think about it, maybe that was when I decided to leave the country and make a life for myself overseas. 'It feels so constricting,' I remember telling Teresa. 'I don't understand,' she replied. 'Never mind,' I said. If I remember rightly, that was the last time we had anything resembling a meaningful conversation. Now I think about it, she knew as well as I did that we always end up playing our parts, as if this city of eight million were a medieval village.

Teresa and I were inseparable growing up but as we slowly made our way into adulthood, our differences gained momentum and ended up separating us. I looked at the clock and decided I would call Lucía as soon as it turned 9 p.m. First though, I would doze a little longer. I padded barefoot to the small CD player on the other side of the room and put on Erik Satie.

* * *

'Wait a sec and I'll go get us a chocolate bar. Oh, and my bag, too, don't want the minxes getting their hands on it,' Susana said to Karen. It was a few hours before Karen went to her place for the first time.

Susana hurried out, leaving the treatment table sprinkled with bread crumbs. Her iPhone beeped with an incoming message. Karen took it between her hands. She didn't mean to read it, but her curiosity won. *If you want sex you can pay for it, but don't treat me bad*, said a message from Susana, then there was a man saying: *Girl, don't be so sensitive, we agreed 1 million and I'll pay it.*

At that moment, Susana came back in and Karen put the phone back where it was.

'Want a Jet bar?' she asked.

'I like the little cards that come inside,' said Karen.

'Me too, I eat one every day to see what it says. Let's see what we have for you today. Oooh, the bat,' Susana laughed, before adopting a ceremonious posture to start reading:

'The bat (Pipistrellus, pipistrellus.) *Bats are the only flying mammals on the planet. Though they appear to have wings like birds, really these are extremely long fingers joined by a membrane that extends to its tail.* Let me see your fingers,' said Susana, taking her hand. 'Yep, it's true. Bat fingers. My mistake, I mean wings: *Contrary to popular belief, bats for the most part don't feed on blood. Some feed on fruit, insects and nectar, and a small percentage feed on animal blood.* Right, from now on I'm calling you Solina.'

'Why Solina?' asked Karen.

'Solina, the shy secretary who turns into a man-eating vampire in *Dracula 2000*.'

'The film?'

'Yes, Solina.'

'I haven't seen it. If you're going to give me a nickname, I prefer Pocahontas.'

'Pocahontas? But that's an Indian name,' Susana said cheerfully.

'Well I'm part Indian, aren't I?' said Karen, taking the last bite of the chocolate bar.

18.

She finished giving Rosario Trujillo a slimming massage, and took no notice when she spoke in English, just as she didn't care when she slipped on her Carolina Herrera overcoat, or when she looked Karen up and down, an expression of disgust on her stretched face.

Karen gave Rosario a broad smile in return for her 5,000-peso tip. She was learning to put on a poker face, was starting to realise that practising the art of falseness made her more likely to win. Rosario Trujillo was one of those women who couldn't spend more than five minutes anywhere before making her superiority felt.

I think Karen was relieved, in a way, once she realised that Rosario acted like that out of insecurity or bitterness; once she understood that she was an unhappy woman, just playing her inevitable part like Karen and all the other actors in this plot. It was like a Shakespeare tragedy where the characters can't escape their destinies, even when they can foresee what's coming; Karen knew that taking one more step would mean plunging into the abyss, but even so she still took it.

But for Lucía, my reading tended to idealise Karen's motives, ennobling them and giving them a fantastical sheen to transform her into a heroine. 'Karen', Lucía said when we started the writing process, 'is the heroine of this story, no doubt about it, but she's a real woman. This is no fairy tale, no epic.' In Lucía's interpretation, Karen stopped viewing Rosario Trujillo as a threat when she started living in the north and working out how she could own the same Carolina Herrera overcoat or Prada handbag, now that these weren't completely out of reach.

In purely pragmatic terms, the major difference between them consisted in that handbag. Well, in the handbag, the coat, the shoes: in a nutshell, in her things. Karen was a good observer.

In those encounters – the two of them sharing the same fifteen square metres behind a closed door, surrounded by the smell of lavender and the sound of New Age music – it was not Rosario Trujillo's naked body that made her superior, it was the price of what that body was clothed in. At least, that's how Karen saw it.

Was it her Bogotan accent, her shrill voice and the intonation she used for servants? Was it because she had a servant, and Karen did not? Was it that way of saying *how is everything?* with a sharp stress on the final syllable and a rising inflection? It didn't matter; the point is that something granted her the right to treat Karen coldly, a privilege Karen would have loved to have at certain moments, because just as all her clients could treat her badly – because they were having a bad day, because that's the way they were, because they felt like it – she always had to turn the other cheek, smile, put up with it, or else look for another job.

That August afternoon, Karen thought about the exchange she'd read on Susana's phone. She wanted to call Emiliano. She thought about the million pesos mentioned. Susana earned in a single weekend the money Karen saved up over eight months and lost in one night. She got out her phone to call Emiliano before her six o'clock appointment. Unlike other times, her mother was affable. She seemed upbeat and told her the interdiction was being processed, which would certify Uncle Juan's psychiatric inability so she could collect his pension. She would have it in a few weeks. That signalled a big change; now her mother would be the one managing the money and her uncle would be dependent on her, not the other way around. She sounded happy. Then she put Emiliano on, and he told a joke Karen didn't understand. He spoke at high speed until he was out of breath. He repeated the joke twice.

'When are you coming, Mamá?' he said finally. It was so long since he'd called her Mamá. When she heard that word, she felt far away.

'Soon, baby, soon.'

'At three?' asked Emiliano.

'I would love to be able to be there at three,' said Karen. 'I'll be there on Monday.'

'Today is Monday,' said Emiliano. Karen was surprised he knew.

Emiliano told her that he was the best at football and he didn't want a bike any more, only some football boots, some good football boots.

'If I have enough saved, I'll get you both for Christmas, sweetheart.'

'That's a long way away. How many *Sponge Bobs* until Christmas?'

'A lot, but time flies.'

'Christmas is a long way away,' Emiliano repeated.

'That's true. It's a long way away, but it will be here before you know it,' said Karen, trying to suppress the thought that the conversation was boring her.

'And my football boots?' he asked again.

'I'll bring some, my love. I promise.'

That afternoon, Karen and Susana left together, as if they'd been colleagues their whole lives. A day after, Karen took her things to Susana's. And that night, while they were settling into the same bed, Karen dared to ask about the exchange she'd read on her phone.

'Well gorgeous,' Susana said, turning out the light. 'I've been working as an escort for the last year.'

'Have you been able to save?' asked Karen, surprised at the ease with which they could talk about this.

'I'm buying this apartment.'

'And how much is it?'

'Three hundred and fifty big ones,' Susana said.

'Can I ask how much you make in a month?'

'In a month? Between eight and ten.'

Karen went quiet. She calculated in a flash: it was eight times what she earned at House of Beauty. It's a deputy minister's salary, I said when she told me.

'And do you have to do awful things?'

'Sometimes, but everything fades.'

'I've only ever been with one man,' Karen said.

Susana laughed.

'You're considering it. Solina. Solina the man-eater. I said that name was a premonition. For the record, it wasn't me, it was the Jet chocolate bar that set you on this course.'

'Hey, there's nothing man-eater about me.'

'Maybe not, but you're scared. I can see fear on you. It's a dark stain in your eyes, it's all over you. You can see it in the way you jump at the slightest thing, in your nervous little laugh, in that tic you have of brushing the hair from your face. What are you going to do to get rid of that fear? You should throw yourself at what makes you feel it, like people who jump back on the horse after they've fallen off.'

Karen was quiet. Susana is psychic, she thought. She knew more about her than she did herself. And even if she didn't think it right that minute when Susana said it, as she watched Rosario Trujillo leave her cubicle later, the memory of Susana's words came back to her with a clarity they lacked before. She fixed her gaze on the 5,000-peso note and it was like when you remember your grandmother's house from your childhood as enormous, but then you go back as an adult and it seems to have shrunk, or more than that, seems trivial, unimportant. That's what happened with her client: once Karen earned enough money that she couldn't care less about her rudeness, Rosario Trujillo began to diminish.

19.

He had pulled down her underwear and had her on the bed, where he was thrusting into her angrily and shouting with a tense, pained expression. Things will never be the same again, she thought. And a blow from Luis Armando made her cheek sting just before he poured more whisky down her throat and stuck his coke-smothered fingers into her mouth.

She was crying. Not half an hour had gone by since she arrived.

When Luis Armando had called, she had imagined a room with white roses, a bubble bath and a glass of champagne, and had thought he would be tender and considerate, that 'there would be nothing she didn't want', a phrase he had uttered several times during their many phone conversations.

At one point, Luis Armando smiled. Like a drowning person spying land, Sabrina smiled back. For a second she thought it was all behind them. But then he pulled away and started laughing. It was as if he were saying, under his breath, 'Got you again.' Sabrina thought about her mamá. She thought about her saying, 'If you don't have something nice to say, don't say anything at all,' but she couldn't think of something nice – not to say, not to keep to herself – just as she would never think of anything, nice or not, ever again.

20.

I n what she would later describe as a waiting room full of fifty-year-old timber furniture being slowly eaten away by weevils, Consuelo Paredes had been waiting for over two hours to see the prosecutor in charge of the case. Another seven people were waiting alongside her, their expressions grim.

'What time did you say he was coming back?'

'He's on his lunch break, please take a seat,' said the secretary, all the while filing her nails.

'But I've been here more than two hours.'

'He must have been delayed.'

Consuelo Paredes saw forensics officers coming and going, heard one shouting to the other: 'Paleta, so was the body willing to cooperate?' The other made a gesture of annoyance: 'Not one fucking bit, and this time I offered it money.' The first laughed half-heartedly.

When the prosecutor finally arrived, he whispered to the secretary, who brought him up to date with what had gone on in his absence. She was in front of a typewriter that took up half of her enormous desk.

The prosecutor turned around and greeted them with a smile and a wave.

'I've got about five minutes each.'

The secretary sent in the four people who arrived before Consuelo Paredes, one after the other. It was almost five o'clock by the time she was called. The whole time, she had been thinking about the right words to use, so she could make the most of the minutes she had with the prosecutor. He was wearing a dung-coloured suit and a cream shirt. His tie was thick and twisted. He was balding, and couldn't be over forty-five.

'How may I help you?'

'My daughter, Sabrina Guzmán, was murdered.'

'Señora, I am so sorry for your loss. But, how shall I put it, if you look at the shelves, all those are cases. They are just this year's, and I can guarantee there are more than five hundred.'

'Excuse me, but that doesn't seem possible,' Consuelo remembers saying to him.

'Señora, if you like, we can spend the five minutes we have together criticising the justice system, or we can talk about the case. Look, here I have everything from a report for stealing a phone, to a hold-up with a knife, a rape and several burglaries, to more phones, more hold-ups and a few murders; it's – how shall I put it? – a diverse lot.'

'But does all of it really have the same importance? Is committing murder the same as stealing a phone?'

'No, Señora, it's not the same, they have different statuses and different protocols. But tell me something, *was* your daughter murdered? We can focus, if you like, Señora.'

'My daughter, Sabrina Guzmán, died on 23 July in unknown circumstances. According to the San Blas Hospital medical report, she died after taking Tryptanol pills, but the autopsy refutes this theory and showed signs of violence – there could even have been sexual violence. And apparently there was a high level of cocaine in her bloodstream …'

'Are you telling me your daughter was raped and there's been a cover-up to hide what happened?'

'Yes,' said Consuelo Paredes.

'One: I can help you get special judicial consent from the Prosecutor's Office to obtain the girl's San Blas medical record. Two: try talking to the doctor, though doctors have the right to uphold confidentiality, so he may opt not to say anything. Three: if you want my advice, get a private investigator.'

'But isn't your office supposed to bring criminals to justice?'

'Very well said, Señora, supposed to. And believe you me, we do the best we can, but look at this office. Do you see a computer? A tablet? No, what you see are five hundred cases filed in paper folders, for which we rely on a very limited, very underpaid forensics team. Señora: work is done to the extent it can be done, but we don't have the time, or the resources. I assure you it is not a question of bad faith. And now, if you will allow me …'

'But could you look at how the case is going? Could you tell me what's happening?'

The prosecutor opened a box he had beneath his desk and dug around in it. After a short while, he took out a folder, opened it, looked at it and said:

'We are establishing the parameters of the investigation to be carried out by forensics.'

'What does that even mean? It's been two months!'

The prosecutor cleared his throat before going on.

'It means an investigative matrix is being established, according to which a methodological agenda will be defined to initiate intelligence work,' he said, raising an eyebrow.

'And when will that be?'

'When will what be, Señora?'

'The intelligence work that will be carried out in accordance with the methodological agenda that's being defined based on the investigative matrix?' said Consuelo Paredes.

The prosecutor hemmed and hawed once more.

'The problem, Señora, is that the medical report thwarted the investigation. If it hadn't been for that, the autopsy would have been performed immediately and time would have been on our side, because it would have been established at once that the cause of death was homicide, you see. Instead, the autopsy was done barely a week ago. Then there is the fact that the autopsy is not conclusive with regards to the cause of the death, as it says that determining such is in the hands of the authorities.'

'Are you telling me it wasn't homicide? You're the ones who should be clearing up whether it was a homicide or not!'

'Exactly!' said the prosecutor with an exaggerated smile. 'Very well, very well, we understand each other, then. First up: establish whether it was a homicide. And only then can this little folder be taken out and given to the homicide unit. Do you follow?'

Consuelo Paredes felt more alone than ever. She realised this was going to be even more difficult than expected.

'How long? How long until you have something, Prosecutor? Until you establish it was a homicide?'

'Give me a week, Señora, just one week, and we'll put you in touch with the forensics officer in charge of the case, so you can discuss these concerns with him. Come back in eight days and I'll have the order to obtain the girl's San Blas medical record. It's a matter of not despairing, and of surrendering to God and praying, Señora, praying a lot.'

'Excuse me, Prosecutor, but could I have your phone number or email address?'

'Certainly,' he said, hemming and hawing once more. After dictating the information, he added in a softer tone: 'I'm so sorry about what you're going through, Señora, but our five minutes were up a while ago.'

21.

Ramelli had been her first client and was fast becoming her best. They saw each other two or three times per week. On a couple of occasions, they ate together. Yet they had never seen each other during the day. So, when he called to invite her to lunch the following Sunday, Karen wondered if he wanted to see her or Pocahontas. Like an interpreter, she was getting better at switching between registers. At House of Beauty, she was still Karen, more so than ever after seeing what happened to Susana, who had been dismissed a couple of weeks earlier after she found her leather jacket stained with hair dye and launched herself at Deisy.

Karen knew that if she was careful, she could maintain her double life for a few months and then leave House of Beauty forever. But that would be when she wanted to, not when she had no choice. Susana's example reminded her to keep her identities separate. Pocahontas showed up with Ferragamo boots and a Massimo Dutti handbag, while Karen still went to House of Beauty wearing her tennis shoes, her hair pulled up in a ponytail.

She leafed through magazines, as focused as a student studying for an exam. What to wear on Sunday? She had started to learn certain codes. Dolce & Gabbana, Armani or Versace were ways of speaking without needing to shout. That night she had a date with a North American who had called her several times the past few weeks. She would have to buy another handbag, as she couldn't always look the same.

The effort she put into playing the part was so intense that she poured all her money into what we might call her characterisation. Her surrender to Pocahontas was such that she forgot she had got into this game so she could bring Emiliano here from Cartagena. More than that, remembering him was growing painful. The person she was when she first came to the city was getting left behind.

After leaving the Santa Lucía apartment, she felt constantly tempted to expose herself to danger, to submit to it and freefall, perhaps so that this time she would be the one controlling the situation.

Karen didn't speak about Wílmer much. Only at the end did we find out that they kept seeing each other. I think her relationship with him caused her so much guilt that she wasn't even able to name it. She left the Laguna Azul motel tired, with 700,000 pesos in cash. She called Wílmer for no more than ten seconds and went on her way. It was early Sunday and the park benches on Calle 59 were occupied by drunks.

John Toll left the motel room a little after Karen; he went in the opposite direction and hailed a taxi off the street, unaware that the driver and accomplices would try to steal his bag and force him on a millionaire's ride to the nearest ATM. Karen wasn't there to hear him shout, or to see him tumble out of the car and run 200 metres before getting three bullets that left him sprawled on the ground, bleeding out.

Her North American client had sweaty hands and apologised for everything. He was so clumsy and insecure in bed. She would never have guessed that he had fought in Iraq and Afghanistan. He liked conventional sex and didn't want her by his side for long, which had suited Karen just fine.

Karen liked this time of day, when night revellers, red eyed and smelling of alcohol, mingled on the same footpath with early risers on their way to the gym. Seeing them together in the same space made her think of a sort of fraternity, even a complicity. It was a concurrence that at any other time of day or night would be impossible.

She wanted to be alone. To close her eyes, eat and cry without feeling observed. And yet, since the rape, she hadn't been able to sleep at night without feeling a rising panic. So, she stayed out until the sun came up, or else she slipped into Susana's bed.

While she walked, she saw a few FOR RENT signs that attracted her curiosity. By the third, she wanted to take a look. It was 22 square metres, dirty and narrow, with the shower head above the bath and a windowless bedroom. The second was a first-floor apartment, also windowless, and was so dark she had to turn on the light to see the palm of her hand. When she decided to look at the third and last before continuing on to her lunch with Ramelli, she crossed her fingers.

The façade was better than anywhere she had lived in Bogotá. It had the same bricks, and beige balconies, like the vast majority of constructions. Like other buildings in the area, this one had never even seen better days. She hadn't let herself believe she was actually looking for a place to live, but when she reached the apartment, she knew what she wanted to say.

A young woman opened the door. She explained to Karen that she and her boyfriend were moving to an apartment where there would be space for their baby, but the contract with the real-estate agent was for three more months.

Karen felt more than satisfied, because three months was the time she needed to save for a bigger apartment, one where there would be space for both Emiliano and her.

It was 40 square metres, with grimy carpet. It had a couple of windows, one in the living room that looked out onto the street and another in the bedroom. The kitchen was open plan and there was a small side table with two chairs, where Karen saw a mug of tea and a history book. The shelves of the bookcase, made with bricks and planks of wood, were crowded with books. Karen went over to peer at them, but didn't find any of Ramelli's.

'I'll take it,' she said, 'I'll take the apartment.'

'But you haven't seen the bathroom yet.'

'I'm still taking it.'

The girl asked her to pay a month in advance and the other two months in November. Karen accepted. The rent was 900,000 pesos, so she took 600,000 out of her handbag and agreed to bring the rest the next day.

The sun was peeking out from behind the hills. She had the impression that things were starting to go well for her, that from that point forward they could only get better.

22.

Consuelo Paredes had spent the past few days in bed. She was tired of dialling the prosecutor's number. It always went to voicemail. She also sent him several emails, but they bounced. Three days before, she'd paid a visit to Cojack of the Cojack and His Detectives agency. The name had caught her attention, as her father had never missed an episode when she was a girl; she thought it could be a sign. The original was spelled with a 'k', not 'c'. In contrast to Kojak, Cojack had hair, which he dyed black. He had a serene manner and acne scarring on his skin. He had chosen his profession and the name of his agency for the New York detective his mother used to swoon over when he watched the series with her as a boy. Like him, he wore a suit and tie and never went out without his hat, though on the webpage he appeared in his old Administrative Department for Security uniform.

On the webpage, the agency offered to hunt down missing persons; to locate debtors so their bank accounts could be frozen; to locate accounts, goods and motor vehicles; to investigate crimes, homicides, scams and thefts; and to perform handwriting analysis.

When Consuelo called, Cojack himself picked up. He said he could see her that afternoon. She took a taxi to the Aquarium Shopping Centre in Chapinero. The office was in a small shop, on the far side of the first floor. The man was sitting on a wooden chair with fabric upholstery, with a few diplomas and photographs of exhumations behind him. There was no computer on the desk, only a scatter of papers, magnifying glasses, a skull, an old camera, several lenses and a box of Tums heartburn relief. Everything looked old and anachronistic, like at the Prosecutor's Office.

Consuelo spoke a long time.

'I'm afraid there might be a real big shot behind all this,' Cojack said, lighting a long, cinnamon-coloured cigarette, just like the ones that the protagonist of the series smoked.

'If someone manages to falsify a medical document in a legal clinic, he's very powerful. We need to search your daughter's things. If you don't mind, tomorrow my men and I will stop by your house and from there we can construct a methodological agenda.'

'I've heard that before,' said Consuelo, disappointed.

'Look here,' said Cojack, opening his eyes wide and pointing at them. 'I left the judicial system because I was sick of the apathy. Everything I know I learned there. And yet, almost everything I've achieved in my forty years in this profession has been as private investigator.'

'Very well, Mr Cojack, or whatever your name is, it was a pleasure to meet you,' said Consuelo, irritated, standing up and holding out her hand.

'Not so fast,' he said. He had the same cavernous, serene voice as the TV detective. Consuelo sat down again, but this time slumped into the chair and burst into uncontrollable weeping.

'You're insensitive,' she cried as smoke contaminated the air around her.

Cojack handed her a box of tissues.

Consuelo blew her nose. Bit by bit her sobs eased.

'My name is Obdulio. Obdulio Cerón.'

Consuelo went quiet. Then she said, calmer now:

'I'd prefer to call you Cojack.'

The man smiled, or so it seemed to her.

'In other words, there will be no justice for my daughter,' Consuelo said.

'Justice, I don't know, but Cojack and His Detectives at least gives you the opportunity to know the truth.'

'That name is ridiculous!'

Cojack continued in a deliberate tone, as if he hadn't heard the insult:

'I daresay that whoever's behind this is an egomaniac. They haven't taken care with the crime scene, yet they don't fear being discovered, either. My bet is that it's one or several powerful people, masters of the universe. Sadly, it's possible it was a night of sex that ended badly.'

'What do you mean?'

'It's a shame the autopsy wasn't done immediately, as we would have had evidence of rape. Now we don't. But there is still that possibility.'

'So how do we find the culprit?'

'First we have to find a suspect. For that to happen, we need to sift through your daughter's things. Once that's done, we can link him to the case.'

'Is it that simple?'

'Sadly, no. If justice isn't on our side, we could come to a dead end.'

'I'm not sure I understand.'

'As the great Sherlock would say, "There is nothing more deceptive than an obvious fact."'

Consuelo looked at her phone. She had to show a client an apartment a few blocks from here. This man – this clown – was her only hope.

'I have to go.'

'I'm leaving, too. If you like, I can come with you and we can keep talking.'

'You still haven't told me your rates.'

'Let me come by tomorrow. After that, we can propose a methodological agenda, and then I'll tell you how much it might cost to follow it. But don't entertain any illusions.'

'Why do you keep insisting it might all come to nothing?'

'Experience, believe me. I've seen cases like this. It can be painful to know the truth, worse than not knowing.'

'That's ridiculous.'

'No, it's not. Truth is necessary when there's justice. But truth with no justice poisons the soul.'

'A philosopher as well as an investigator,' said Consuelo, getting to her feet.

Cojack took his coat and hat from the rack and motioned for Consuelo Paredes to follow him.

23.

From the terrace of Upper Side restaurant, where he was waiting for Karen, Ramelli noticed a corpulent man coming towards him. He looked about forty and had *Happiness Is You* in hand.

'Are you Eduardo Ramelli?'

'I sure am,' he replied with a smile, lifting his sunglasses and setting them on his shiny, ash-coloured hair.

'What an honour! You have no idea how important this book has been for me.'

'I'm so happy to hear that, that's what it's all about,' said Ramelli, nervous.

'I'm with my girlfriend. Can I tell her to come over? She started with *I Love Myself* and she was the one who told me about your work. Truth is, it's changed my life …'

'That's what it's about, isn't it?' repeated Ramelli, distracted as he saw Karen approaching the table.

She was looking beautiful. Sensual and elegant at the same time, he thought. The corpulent man's girlfriend came over and arrived a few seconds before Karen did. Karen felt Eduardo's eyes running over her.

'I can't believe it!' the young woman said, putting her hands on her face.

Ramelli smiled again.

'I love it when you talk about being a river that flows … it's something I try to do every day.' She had gone red and was blinking.

Karen stayed behind the rosy-cheeked woman, unsure whether to sit down or wait.

Ramelli said something about awakening the soul, got to his feet and gave her an exaggerated hug.

'Take a seat, please.'

Then he took the copy of *Happiness Is You* from the man's hands, which were hairy as well as chubby, and asked who he should dedicate it to.

'This is a sign, don't you think?' the woman said to her boyfriend, laughing. 'Look, Master, I had really low self-esteem, but after reading *I Love Myself* that changed. I started to understand that I could have everything I wanted in life, so long as I accepted myself for who I am, limitations and all. And that was when I found love.'

Ramelli kept a fixed, exaggerated smile on his face.

The couple looked out of place. Their outdated clothes, excess weight and kind-heartedness clashed with the surroundings. Karen looked around. They were sitting on a fourth-floor terrace with a view of Zona Rosa. The chairs were transparent acrylic, and the tables were metal. Inside, enormous red chandeliers, also acrylic, hung from high ceilings. The place was painted white, and large photos of New York decorated the walls. While Eduardo said farewell to his admirers, Karen looked over the menu, which was mostly in English: suckling pig spring rolls, pepper steak, baked potato, NoLIta-style soup, Manhattan-style burgers, lobster mini pizzas, Waldorf salad, tandoori chicken. She didn't understand anything. She looked at the French people at the next table, whose meals looked delicious, but she didn't know what those meals were called, or how to pronounce any of it. Finally, the couple left. Eduardo looked at her with his pool-blue eyes. He took her by the hand and squeezed her palm rhythmically, not saying anything, looking at her all the while. She felt a tingling throughout her body. This was the closest she'd come to a romantic date in her life. Then Eduardo's phone sounded and he jumped up and said:

'I'm sorry, I have to take this call.'

He held the phone up to his ear.

'Brother! To what do I owe this pleasant surprise?'

Karen caught a squeaky voice on the other side speaking loudly, but the words were unintelligible.

'Is it serious?' asked Ramelli. 'Thank you, brother, I'll keep on top of it while you head to Barranquilla. We'll have to organise an emergency plan. No, not now. I'll call you later, brother. But don't worry, we'll handle it.' He hung up.

'Is everything all right?' asked Karen.

The waiter came over and asked if they were ready to order.

Karen looked at the menu again, now a little anxious.

'The hamburger, please,' she said, handing the waiter the menu.

'Would you like the *bacon burger* or the *cheese burger?*' He said the names in English.

'The *bacon burger*,' she said. 'Could I have that with cheese please? And no bacon?'

Eduardo smiled at her.

'It would be our pleasure,' replied the waiter, not correcting her.

Eduardo asked for the suckling pig spring rolls as a starter and a BLT sandwich for the main. To drink, he wanted a gin and tonic. Karen asked for a Coca-Cola and then felt ridiculous for ordering as if she were a nine-year-old.

'Do you like it here?' asked Eduardo.

'It's elegant,' said Karen shyly.

'Isn't it?' said Ramelli. 'The food is nothing special, but the idea is that you feel like you're in a *top cocktail bar*, like the ones you see in London, New York or Paris, you know?'

Karen nodded. She looked at the vertical gardens on the rooftop. In the area out the back, there were leather couches and wooden tables and a bar lined with stools. The sky was the same blue as Ramelli's eyes. For a moment, she imagined sharing a life with him; a life where there would be space for Emiliano, a house, a dog, and maybe a property in the lowlands where they could spend the weekends.

The waiter filled their glasses with water. Eduardo broke his silence:

'Look. I barely know you. This must be, what, the sixth time I've seen you, but I feel like I've known you all my life.'

The waiter served the suckling pig spring rolls and Eduardo took a large bite. He concentrated on savouring the pastry-wrapped pork. His mouth still full, he said that it was perfectly cooked, before grumbling over the sweet-and-sour sauce. For Karen, this precise moment was just like that sauce, bittersweet. She wasn't sure how to take Eduardo's abrupt move from a declaration of love to the flavours of some rolls of meat. She maintained her smile and her silence. And Eduardo had forgotten her name, or at least he hadn't pronounced it.

'You know I call you Pocahontas out of affection, gorgeous,' he said, winking at her.

After all, he was the Master, Karen told herself, wanting to think that everything he did had a deeper meaning, a logic that escaped her. The mains were served and Eduardo kept talking about food. Now he told her about the different places in Bogotá where you could eat Peking duck. The declaration of love had completely left his mind.

'The best by far is Thai Ching Express,' continued Ramelli.

She didn't want to admit that she was starting to get bored. Eduardo went on about Chinese, Thai and Vietnamese food for a good quarter of an hour, and about the restaurants in Bogotá where that kind of food was available, as well as ranking them for price and quality.

The corpulent couple came over again. This time the woman had red eyes and her cheeks were rosier than before.

'I didn't want to leave without thanking you again, Master,' she said to Ramelli. 'Bumping into you here is a sign.'

The man next to her nodded vehemently.

The woman had a red coat and the same colour lipstick. She continued: 'See, my baby proposed to me today' – and on saying this she let out a deep sigh – 'precisely today. Can you believe it?'

'Unbelievable,' said Eduardo, taking a long sip of his gin and tonic.

'It's a sign,' insisted the woman, 'a sign I never would have recognised if I hadn't read your work. Dear Master, allow me to invite you to our wedding.'

'It would be the greatest honour,' chimed in the corpulent man; 'but how rude of us … we haven't introduced ourselves. Alfredo Largacha, proctologist at your service.'

He extended his hand.

Ramelli took it, after eyeing it more carefully than is usually appropriate.

'Gloria Motta, bacteriologist,' the woman said, holding out her hand too.

'You two are made for each other,' said Eduardo with the same tense smile.

After hearing that the wedding would take place in the Cachipay municipality, Ramelli promised to do everything he could to celebrate with them, but said he thought he remembered a trip around that date. Doctor Largacha gave him his card, 'because you never know when you'll need a proctologist,' and winked. Ramelli, in response, introduced Karen, who even out of the corner of his eye looked ravishing. On noting how the doctor ogled her, he couldn't resist saying:

'This is Karen, my girlfriend.'

Karen almost choked on a French fry. She felt red and shy but managed to rise and shake the couple's hands.

At the end of lunch, washing a fried ice cream down with a double espresso, Ramelli remembered his earlier pronouncement.

'Where was I? Ah, yes ... after living my life, not knowing where it was going, and always living each moment with no thought for the future, someone came along who took my breath away, and that someone is you ...'

Eduardo kept talking as he repeated the rhythmic movement and soft squeeze of her hand, looking at her intensely.

Two days later, while Karen was on a bus, she recognised his words in Carlos Vives's song 'Aventurera'.

But for the time being she didn't want to think of Ramelli as a fraud, she wanted to let herself get carried away by the romance, to feel like an enraptured fifteen-year-old girl. On the terrace of that nondescript restaurant Ramelli stroked her face and kissed her deeply, as if they were smitten teenagers.

Just before they stepped into the lift – Karen floating rather than walking, despite the eight-centimetre heels torturing her feet; he with his arm wrapped firmly around her waist so that she felt like a princess – they bumped into a man with an aquiline nose and chest hair.

'Doctor, a pleasure to see you,' said Eduardo.

'Likewise, Master,' replied the doctor.

'This is my girlfriend,' said Ramelli, and Karen greeted him, this time not blushing.

'My pleasure. Karen Valdés.'

'Roberto Venegas,' the doctor said.

In the lift, Karen asked, 'Is that your doctor?'

'No, darling. He's one of my employees at Health Cross, the healthcare provider that my associate and I own.'

'You own a healthcare provider?'

'Yes, can you believe it?'

'You do so much,' she said, intent on pleasing him and being his Sunday girlfriend. 'Are you taking me for a stroll?' And she took his hand.

'If by stroll you mean a stroll among the clouds. But first: I've got a surprise for you.' He took a package out of the back of the car. Carolina Herrera, she read on the bag. She needed no more words or gestures to feel this was true and pure love.

24.

Karen told us a good part of what happened in those months, but she always omitted Wilmer – I'm not sure whether deliberately or because her subconscious silenced her memory of him, the only man she sought out who wasn't a client.

Lucía, however, thinks Karen kept a lot of things quiet. And looking back, I suppose she was used to omitting details when she talked about herself. To preserve only the good memories, perhaps her mind suppressed what was painful. The day she spoke about her fifteenth birthday party, for example, she failed to mention having her hair chemically straightened for the first time, or the pain it caused her.

It was weeks later when she broached the subject. She was giving me a massage. Lying on the treatment table, I scratched my head several times. I said that those Pantene products irritated my scalp, that my hair was greasy and I had to wash it daily. Karen seemed absent for a moment, didn't make any comment about it and then, suddenly, as she worked a knot out of my back, she started to speak:

'The first time I had my hair relaxed was for my fifteenth birthday party. My mamá explained that if I scratched, I would hurt myself. When I get nervous, I always scratch my head. I've never felt any pain like it. My scalp broke out in sores.'

'I like curls,' I said. 'You've never let them grow out?'

'When I was little. At school, they said I looked like a monkey. They made orang-utan sounds at me and other girls who had Afros. Some girls were sent to school with their hair straightened, even really little ones.'

'What about your mamá?'

'She's had hers relaxed since I can remember. She does it religiously, every two months; it's a ritual for her. Like the women who come here: every two weeks they have a wax, every eight days a manicure, every month a facial, every three weeks fake eyelashes ... Not to mention the cosmetic treatments, the laser hair removal, the Botox, there are so many things nowadays. Out of everything, I never miss a wax or straightening my hair. It's a pain, not only because it hurts, but because it smells like rotten eggs. Your eyes sting. In Cartagena, women know all about it. They use hair irons, rollers, hair wraps; they tame the wildest curls. Nixon used to say it was an insult to our ancestors. I don't know about that. I only know I don't like to see a dishevelled black woman in the mirror. I believed Nixon for a while. What he said made sense to me. If God made me, curly hair and all, why contradict Him? I went to church then, almost as often as I got my hair relaxed. Then I stopped getting it done, but because I'd been doing it for four years, my hair didn't spring back curly right away; it went all weird, like a wire-bristle broom. I felt ugly, then I got pregnant and I was sad. I couldn't stand seeing myself in the mirror. Nixon made a point of calling me black, but I'd never thought about it before, hadn't thought of myself as black. I'd maybe thought of my mamá as black – I always laughed inwardly when she said she was "cinnamon coloured" because she's black as shoe polish. But me? I have a different skin colour; I'm the one who's almost cinnamon-coloured; perhaps the blackest thing about me is this unruly, kinky hair. On TV, they always talk about shiny, silky, smooth hair, and none of that describes a black person's hair. Afros are for people in El Pozón shanties, that's what my mamá taught me from when I was little; for people who live in dumps or puddles, with no work, no papers, no house. That's what I was taught to believe, so when Nixon called me black and read me Jorge Artel poems, I felt a warmth inside, a pride I never knew, about something that usually embarrassed me. I know I'm beautiful, or at least really hot. I know how men look at me, how they want me, but I also know that if I had an Afro the same men who would show me off like a prize they won in the lottery would find themselves suddenly embarrassed. When I get called an Indian, it doesn't bother me so much. After all, there's Pocahontas, who is beautiful, and she's the star of a Disney film. Do I look black to you, Doña Claire? I think I'm pretty much the same colour as President Obama, with a white person's features and a black person's hair. My hair has been my cross to bear. I hate the smell of those chemicals. Sometimes they make me retch, and as the years go by I hate them even more. But despite that, I'd never have it in me to stop using them. When I got pregnant, I told myself that I at least needed to feel like I was beautiful. At the end of the day, feeling beautiful and having straight hair are one and the same for me.'

I didn't say anything. I knew Karen straightened her hair, but had never imagined the torment behind it.

Karen massaged my calves, then spent a moment on my feet, seemingly lost in thought.

'Nixon thought differently,' she said suddenly. 'If more of us were like Nixon, maybe we would be better off. In all honesty, I don't like the look of Afros. Nothing I can do about that. Imagine, there was a beautiful young black woman in my neighbourhood: she let her hair grow out in an Afro and do you think she could find a job? She was beautiful, and educated, but no one wanted that disorder in their office, on their premises, in their shop, and much less in their beauty salon. Mamá would watch her go by and say, "One of these days I'm going to come snip off that hair of yours, and I'll make myself a pillow out of it." I would laugh. The girl studied some weird degree. Sociology, I think it was. She tried to bring people together, same as Nixon, to speak about pride and our ancestors and whatnot, and, in one of those meetings, a lady who washed clothes for a living stood up and said to her: "And has so much pride and pain got you a job?" Everyone burst out laughing. I felt sorry for the girl because she was onto something. You shouldn't discriminate against people because of their hair, I understand that, but I also agree that an Afro doesn't look good in an office. Anyway, she left the neighbourhood. We didn't hear any more about her. She had rented a place at a neighbour's, but stayed barely a few months. Maybe it wasn't the place for her. Sometimes I remember her, though I forget her name. I hope someone gave her a job, so she didn't have to get that hair of hers straightened. For her, more than the pain and annoyance of hair straightening, it would have been the fact that she had succumbed finally that would have been the real trauma. Could you turn over, Doña Claire?'

I stared at her, at her lovely features. Her lips seemed fuller than usual. I imagined what her hazel eyes would look like at night. I wanted to kiss her. I wanted to, but instead I kept still, perfectly still. I tried to control the rhythm of my breathing. I closed my eyes. I wanted Karen's massage never to end, wanted her voice – the voice that sounded in my ears when I tossed and turned at night, unable to fall asleep – to murmur sweet nothings in my ear, softly, slowly, with her rhythmic and playful cadence, her low voice, with that flavour, that tongue.

25.

It was three in the afternoon on a Tuesday and the public servants were wearing party hats. They were cutting up a cake smothered in Chantilly cream and the cleaner, who was also wearing a party hat, was giving out Colombiana cola in little plastic cups.

'Excuse me,' said Consuelo, raising her voice to make herself heard above the loud music. 'I would like to know if the prosecutor is in.'

'He's not here, because of the long weekend. He'll be back tomorrow.'

'Isn't the long weekend over today?'

'He must have taken the day off, I'm not sure,' said the secretary, visibly annoyed. 'I'm not secretary to him alone.'

'Could you give me his mobile number?'

'No, Señora, I can't. I'm not authorised.'

'But he said he would put me in touch with the forensics officer taking on the case, so we could speak about … He said he would be in today.'

'What about your lawyer?' the secretary asked.

'Come again?'

'They usually deal with the case lawyers, not with the families. Submit a writ. It's really hard to get looked after if you have no writ. Can't you see he has like five hundred cases in his office?'

'But the prosecutor told me that—'

'He deals with a lot of people, he can't take charge of everything,' said the secretary, lifting the cup of Colombiana to her mouth.

'And he didn't leave an order requesting my daughter's medical record from San Blas?'

'No, Señora, he didn't leave me anything – anything at all,' said the secretary, hurriedly backing away because her colleagues had lit the candles and were waiting to sing 'Happy Birthday'.

Consuelo followed her and said the prosecutor must have made a mistake when he jotted down his phone number; it always went to voicemail.

'No way, hun. *Sorry*,' she added in English.

That afternoon, Consuelo Paredes called her ex-husband and told him about Cojack and her two visits to the Prosecutor's Office. Against her expectations, he reacted positively to the idea of hiring the investigator, and even offered to help with the fees. He also agreed to help search for a competent lawyer to speed up the process. Consuelo told him about the progress Cojack and his men, who appeared to be his nephews, had made. They had been in the apartment and turned Sabrina's room upside down.

'Did they find anything?'

'A note written on a page ripped from her exercise book.'

'What did it say?'

'"Did you know there are more than thirty kinds of kisses? And we've barely tried one. Wait for me to come back, and I'll show you the other twenty-nine,"' Consuelo read out.

'Revolting,' said Jorge Guzmán. 'And was it signed?'

'No, but it's initialled L.A.D.'

'L.A.D.?' asked Jorge Guzmán.

'No idea,' said Consuelo.

'Do you think this is the killer?'

'Who knows, but this note could be useful.'

'Let's find out who this L.A.D. is.'

Consuelo was happy to go along with that. She started to tell her ex-husband about the San Blas Hospital visit and the follow-up matrix that Cojack devised but he interrupted:

'I think it would be best if we spoke about these things in person, you never know.'

'You never know what?'

'If someone's listening. For now, we've said enough. Let's meet up tomorrow. Stay calm. We'll get some-where; we have to.'

'Jorge, what did they do to our little girl?'

He didn't answer. It took a couple of seconds for Consuelo to realise he was crying.

26.

A dull blow to her ribs, like a stab wound, pulled her mind back into the room.

'Do whatever I say,' said Luis Armando, who had transformed into a strange thing, a monster who knew how to hit, who knew how and where to land his blows so that they left little evidence: only his victim's pain.

'But cut out that frightened expression, it puts me off,' he said while searching for the roll of paper to snort another line.

'What are you doing?' Sabrina dared to ask when he started rubbing cocaine on her vulva.

'Spoiling you.'

The last thing Sabrina thought was that everything was her fault. She didn't get to know the person who was now hurling her from one place to another, who was using her body to unload his rage at the world. For her, he was a soft voice, a voice that made her feel special. An elegant, refined man who found her beautiful. And sweet. *Beautiful and sweet*, he said to her that time in Unicentro when he bought her a hamburger. A guy who owned a BMW SUV. *And sexy*, he added the second time they saw each other, one month later. That day he was gentle when he kissed her, and twice he asked if she was a virgin. Were all men monsters when it came to intimacy? Sabrina knew they couldn't all be. Her father wasn't a monster. He was a good man. Thinking about her father crushed her, and the urge to urinate she'd been feeling for a while now grew almost unbearable. The pain returned, leaving little room for thought. She wouldn't get the chance to think about how she would never do all the things she had imagined, that she would never know love, would never be a mother, would never study gastronomy, would never live abroad. She would die without realising she would never see her mother or brother again, wouldn't attend her graduation party, wouldn't see Los Angeles, try marijuana, or feel once more that she was the sexiest woman alive, or make peace with her father, whom she had never forgiven for divorcing her mother and forming another family.

Now Sabrina knew she had been unfair. Relationships end. One day the love is gone and it's no one's fault. Her father had a woman by his side, that was good. Now she saw this. It seemed like Luis Armando was moving at an impossible speed; she sensed him climbing the walls to the ceiling and back down to the floor. She let out a silly little laugh. She couldn't feel anything any more, or she could, but she didn't care. Maybe if her mamá had been more willing to talk. Maybe if Sabrina hadn't been an idiot. She tried to follow Luis Armando's instructions: faster, slower, more rhythmically, imagine a Bom Bom Bum lollipop, no, an ice cream, rub your hand up and down, but faster, no, not so fast, you're so rough, it would be better if you got the hell out of this fucking room, and Sabrina thought the nightmare was almost over – once out in the hallway, everything would be over, she would just have to go downstairs and request a taxi, a telephone, call her mamá – and she would never go out with a guy like him again (no more strangers, no more psychopaths dressed as heart-throbs), but then the 'never again' took an unexpected twist and he grabbed her by the throat. She let out a few tears, couldn't cry out, couldn't do anything. He lifted her off her feet and said she'd never know how to make a man happy, that her feeble child's body was a joke. Sabrina wanted to get away but she felt weak. Luis Armando kept up his game. He flipped her over as if she were a doll, threw her by her hair, twisted her one way then the other. She couldn't put up a fight, couldn't cry any more, thought she was dead, thought it was a relief to have died finally (she had expected to die the first time she wished for it), guessed she had been in the room over an hour now, knew no one was coming to save her. It no longer mattered. She closed her eyes. Her heart was about to explode. She was bleeding. She didn't know where from, but she was bleeding. A viscous warmth somewhere, maybe between her legs. She wasn't sure. All that blood, she thought. I'm no longer a virgin, she said to herself. Not any more. She remembered the white gloves they wore at school. 'Symbol of purity,' the principal often said. She didn't see him swiftly get dressed, nimbly tie his shoelaces and knot his tie, as if this had all been a masterful performance and he wasn't drunk, or drugged, or crazy. She didn't see him splash water on his face. She didn't see him sit on the bed and call his papá. She didn't hear him say what had happened, nor hear his father say that Ramelli would take care of it, to stay calm. She didn't see herself with mouth open, terror in her eyes, as if she had spent her whole life suspended in a scream. She wasn't privy to any of this because, after fearing it so long, after wishing for it, Sabrina was dead.

27.

For Diazgranados, a psychoanalyst was not so different from a speech therapist or a nutritionist. Claire Dalvard had studied in Paris, so he told himself that maybe she would have techniques to help him lose fifty kilos that wouldn't require that he stop eating. But what really made him call her was that question about his son. Aníbal had asked Luis Armando if he had a colleague called Aline and his son had said he didn't know the name. So why had that doctor, who by all appearances had no link to him or his family, lied to get information about his son? He made an appointment. But after making it, he got his men to follow her. That's how he found out that one of the places she most often visited was House of Beauty, where, coincidentally, his wife was also a regular.

Then he found out that both Claire and his wife saw a beautiful young woman called Karen Valdés, the hooker who Ramelli treated like a girlfriend. Once bitten, twice shy; he knew he would have to be vigilant. What could that girl know about what went down? Didn't the newspapers state that one of the last things Sabrina Guzmán did before she died was go to a beauty salon in Zona Rosa? What if it was the same salon? And what if Claire,

Karen, his wife and the dead girl were connected in that place, off limits to men, where there was room for all kinds of conspiracies and secrets?

It was just past seven in the evening. Mondays were usually busy at House of Beauty, but today had been especially quiet. Karen wanted to talk to Susana, to tell her she was moving out. She felt like talking, like stretching out on the couch and chatting with her friend. She wasn't seeing any clients that night. On her way back to the apartment she bought a tub of ice cream. It would be their last night under the same roof; they'd have a nice time. Yet she only needed to take one step inside to see things weren't as she had imagined. Despite how small the space was, she couldn't see to the other side because of the smoke. Lying on the sofa, Susana was watching the reality show *Protagonistas de Novela*. The room stank of weed. Karen greeted Susana, but she didn't respond.

She put the ice cream in the freezer, then sat down beside her, but Susana didn't take her eyes off the screen. A group of men and women were coming and going, wearing black shirts stamped with their names. Karen read 'Júver', 'Yina', 'Everly', 'Omar' and 'Ana María'. She moved closer to her friend. Yina, poured into embroidered jeans, with hair extensions, false eyelashes and blue eyeliner, said to Júver: 'What a traitorous bitch, voting to have her best friend thrown out of the house.' In the next scene, Júver was sticking his tongue in Ana María's ear.

'How are you?' tried Karen.

'Watching this,' said Susana as she dragged on the end of a joint.

'This show's awful.'

Susana's initial reply was to turn up the volume.

'You don't have to watch it if you don't want,' she said finally, and Karen smelled alcohol in the air.

'Could I have a sip of your Coca-Cola?'

'Pour yourself one, there's more in the kitchen.'

'I just want a sip.' Karen took the glass. 'Yum, that's good rum.'

'I know what you're trying to do,' said Susana.

Karen turned off the TV just when Andrea Serna was saying: 'And up for eviction this week is ...' Susana stood up, angry.

'I offer you my home, I open the door for you to a well-paid job – a job that will change your life – and you show up here, judging me as if you're better.'

'If the job will change my life, I hope it won't change me like it's changed you.'

'What's that supposed to mean?'

'You're drinking too much. You're drunk all the time ... and stoned.'

'So what?'

'It's no good for you.'

'And what's good for me, in your opinion, Little Miss Butter-Wouldn't-Melt-In-My-Mouth?'

Karen didn't say anything. Susana turned on the

TV. *Protagonistas de Novela* had finished. A voice said: 'Guerrilla, demobilise, your family awaits you,' and there was a green field with sunflowers, a blue sky in the background, and children running through the grass.

'I'm leaving,' said Karen.

'Off you go.'

'No, I'm serious, I'm leaving. I found an apartment and I'm moving in tomorrow. I've already paid October's rent.'

'What about Emiliano? What about your dream of bringing him here to live with you? I knew it, I knew you were full of shit. Face it. You've spent years telling yourself lies. You're no better than me, and you've already forgotten your son.'

Karen slapped her.

Susana stared at her. 'How much did it cost you to rent the apartment? I've said we could make room for Emiliano here, that I'd help.'

'There's no space here,' Karen said quickly.

'And there is space where you're going? You've got a room for him? Or did you spend the money for a two-bedroom apartment on boots and handbags?'

Karen didn't answer, just took Susana's address book and the cordless phone, and shut herself in the bathroom.

'You're a hooker! Accept it! A slut, a gold-digger, now you only want to have nice things, *bitch*!' screamed Susana, banging on the bathroom door.

Full of fury, Karen searched for 'M' in her friend's address book. She found the number for Susana's mother – Karen had never laid eyes on her, but she'd heard her on the phone with her daughter. She dialled the number she found, waited for it to ring twice, three times.

'Hello?'

'Is this Susana's mother?'

'Yes, who is this?'

'I'm Karen Valdés, your daughter's friend.'

'Has something happened to Susy?' asked the voice on the other end.

'Yes, Señora. She's had a relapse. She's drinking too much, taking drugs, talking nonsense, she's out of control. She might have to be admitted,' added Karen slowly. 'I'm really sorry. I've done everything I can, Señora, but your daughter's unwell and I can't help her any more.'

When Karen came out of the bathroom, Susana had left. The TV was still on. Karen packed her things as fast as she could and got out of there.

28.

It had been years since she'd done a manicure and pedicure, but today she had to do at least four. Dilia hadn't shown up, so her appointments had been shared out among everyone else.

Crouching, Karen filed down Doctor Del Castillo's corns with a pumice stone. Beside him, his wife, Señora María Elvira, was being taken care of by Nubia, House of Beauty's longest-serving beautician. On her other side was Señora María Elvira's friend, Doña Elena.

Karen looked at those dry feet with greenish nails. It was rare for a man to come into House of Beauty. She wondered what Doctor Del Castillo's penis looked like. The thought made her squeamish and she tried to shake herself free of it.

'Yes, honey, it's a real shame, truly. You're young, you should leave this country, start over elsewhere. This "New Colombia" – all these people with money who have come from who knows where – it's growing all the time,' Doña Elena was saying to Señora María Elvira.

'At least the Country Club crowd are still people like us. But look, this problem with the nouveau riche is happening all over the world.'

'True,' said Doña Elena.

'And then there's all this terrible violence.'

'These days, simply taking a taxi is a terrible risk – you may as well throw yourself from the fifth floor.'

'Didn't you hear the news this morning? A man came out of one of those Chapinero motels on Sunday morning and when some men tried to take him on a millionaire's ride and he resisted, they put three bullets into him,' said Doctor Del Castillo.

'Ah, yes,' says Doña María Elvira, who seemed to know everything. 'John Toll, the DEA agent. On Twitter, they said the poor thing didn't survive. What a shame! He was so lovely looking, a blond fellow …'

Karen felt like throwing up, but held it back. She saw three feet instead of one. She steadied herself and breathed deeply, like I'd told her. She concentrated on her breaths, in and out. She tried to count to a hundred, as I'd recommended she did when she felt a panic attack coming on. She tried to imagine she was in the countryside. There were still three feet instead of one. She didn't get past ten.

'Oh my, how embarrassing for our international standing,' said Doña Elena. 'That's why others see us as they do.'

'What a heartache of a country,' added Doña María Elvira.

'We need to round up those reprobates and give them what they deserve,' said Doctor Del Castillo. 'Do you know the details?'

'He resisted handing over his bag, so they shot him three times. He was bleeding out on the pavement when a good Samaritan took him to San Ignacio Hospital, but as they were arriving he bled to death, the poor guy ...'

'And that happened where?'

'In that little park on Calle 59: imagine.'

'An outrage,' said Doctor Del Castillo.

Karen wondered if some other gringo could have left a motel in Chapinero and crossed the park on Calle 59 in the early hours of Sunday morning, someone different from the John who handed her an envelope containing 700,000 pesos.

'And what was he doing in Chapinero at that time of the morning?'

'Must have been with a hooker. There are all those motels there,' said Doña María Elvira.

Just then, Karen lost control of the nail cutters. Doctor Del Castillo let out a yelp.

'Could the hooker be an accomplice in the robbery?' asked María Elvira, ignoring her husband's cry.

'Ouch! Careful, my girl, I'm not all dead yet!' said the doctor. 'The poor woman: being a hooker doesn't make her a murderer.'

A few drops of blood ran in the water.

'Well excuse me, but a prostitute is no saint,' said Doña María Elvira.

'The poor family,' added Doña Elena.

'Poor things,' echoed Doña María Elvira. 'Did you know he fought in Afghanistan, only to die by the hand of a savage Indian in Bogotá? It's so unfair.'

'Excuse me,' Karen barely managed to get out. She ran to the lavatory. She threw up. Then she put down the lid and sat down. Her head was going around in circles. She tried to think. For a second she wanted to call Wílmer, to ask him if he did it. She had a bad feeling. She got up. She went down to the second floor, not giving any explanation to Doctor Del Castillo, who looked on, his mouth open. She went into her cubicle, found Consuelo Paredes's card in her wallet and dialled.

'*Luis Armando Diazgranados*, Doña Consuelo. That's who your daughter was seeing the day she came here for a wax.'

'Who is this?' said Consuelo Paredes, sounding shocked.

'It's Karen, from House of Beauty.'

'What do you mean?' said Consuelo Paredes, almost shouting. 'Why didn't you say so earlier? What else do you know? Tell me!'

'I don't know. I have a bad feeling about this. Please don't say I told you. If anything happens to me in future, get in touch with Claire Dalvard, you can find her number through the Colombian Psychoanalytic Society.'

'L.A.D.,' said Consuelo to herself.

'What was that?' asked Karen.

'Forget it. Look, thank you for this.'

Hanging up, Karen wondered again if she should call Wilmer. She wavered. She dialled his number and it rang, but no one answered.

29.

J orge Guzmán hired a lawyer who knew how to guarantee that, in just a few days, an agent would be working on the investigation. They had a list of interviews to conduct: with two of Sabrina's friends, with the doctor who wrote the death certificate, and with Karen Valdés, who was possibly the last person to see her alive. A facial composite sketch of the taxi driver who dropped Sabrina at the hospital was being circulated at the police stations. In addition to this, and armed with a court order, they started inquiring at hotels on the north side of the city, showing a photo of Sabrina and asking if anyone had seen her. They also searched the hotel registry books for her name, but as they suspected she'd used an alias, they didn't expect this to come to anything. As for the autopsy, since almost three weeks passed between her death and it being performed, it wasn't possible to find DNA or semen matches. Cojack had put some work into tracking down a sample of Luis Armando Diazgranados's handwriting, to see if it matched the note found in Sabrina's bedroom. After various phone calls and false starts, he had succeeded in arranging a meeting with the estate agent who had managed the purchase of a property Luis

Armando owned in New Hope. With a little persuasion, Cojack had secured a photocopy of the title deed, signed at the bottom by Luis Armando Diazgranados. According to Cojack's calculations, it would be a couple of weeks before the handwriting analysis was ready. If the signature matched the note sent to Sabrina, they could link this to the case and put in a request to trace his calls for the past six months, and to have him followed. The DNA test would have been the most compelling evidence, but only if the autopsy had taken place ten days earlier. Even so, the process was underway. For the first time in almost four months, Consuelo Paredes and Jorge Guzmán didn't feel utterly defeated.

30.

It was 31 October, her birthday. As a special treat, Lucía had bought a chocolate-filled pastry, and was eating it now with a bowl of strawberries. She was flipping through the paper when a picture of Eduardo took her by surprise. It wasn't like the article she'd read a couple of months before, when Health Cross was singled out as one of the corrupt health-service providers; this time, Eduardo Ramelli, as the company's legal representative, was being accused of robbing state resources. She read the article and, before she could finish, her telephone sounded and wouldn't stop. Yet it wasn't people calling to wish her a happy birthday, but people annoyed by what had been written, calling to express their solidarity with Ramelli. She heard phrases such as, 'That rag should be shut down for printing lies,' or, 'We know Eduardo would never do something like that,' using a plural that Lucía found confusing because she didn't know whom it included. Even Lucía's mother called and hurried out the happy birthday to tell her she would always stand by her in hard times, an old chestnut that Lucía interpreted as a gesture of solidarity towards her ex-husband more than towards her. In a confident tone, her mother concluded: 'They should lock up those journalists for defamation.' Lucía opted to remain silent. She was about to turn off her phone when my call came through.

'How are you?' I asked.

Lucía started crying.

'Want me to come over?'

'Hurry,' she said.

Lucía looked at her surroundings and felt estranged from them. The things that had accompanied her all her life now seemed to belong to someone else. So did she herself, so did her very life. She was angry. She couldn't work out why she'd made the decisions she had. It was too late to reinvent herself, she thought. It was fifty-seven years too late to start again.

I took her a box of chocolates and a woollen blanket. Lucía made tea. I got there quickly, considering the traffic, and found her in a sweatshirt, her face red and her nose stuffy.

'How are you?' I asked again, now looking into her eyes.

Lucía took a chocolate from the box and stared at it a moment before lifting it to her mouth.

'Do you think it's true?' I asked.

'Yes,' said Lucía, looking elsewhere. Then she added, 'Life is a fabrication, don't you think? Something we make up from start to finish. Even those supposedly happy times that give it meaning are pure fiction.'

After saying this, she devoured a chocolate in one bite.

'Another?' I asked.

'No way. Pour me a whisky.'

It didn't seem right to point out that it was Tuesday, and only ten in the morning. I opened the cabinet drawers until I found the bottle, searched for a glass, poured her a drink to the brim and handed it to her.

'You're not having one?' she asked.

'I've got a patient at one this afternoon.'

But after saying that, I got to my feet again and poured myself a glass, though a little less generously.

'I used to be interested in the world … You know, at one time I had an uncommon curiosity for the smallest things. The life of mites, fleas …'

Lucía took a long swig of whisky.

'I think Papá always saw me as an intelligent woman, but in his head my main role was to get married to someone important, maybe a minister. I seemed so mild and gentle to him. He would say to my mamá: "Lucía is so mild and gentle. She's going to marry well." That surprised me, coming from a man like him.'

'What's this about fleas?'

'I found them interesting. I could have been a biologist, an expert in the reproductive organs of cockroaches, for example.'

'Well. Perhaps.'

'Eduardo's no longer with me, it's true, but neither am I. Do you get my meaning? There's nothing left in the place where I was, Claire. Just this old and ugly body, these broken desires from a simple life, with a few blazes of happiness. I've always looked for approval, Claire. That's been my weakness. If only I could have my life again.'

Lucía took another sip of whisky.

'Are you angry?'

'I don't know,' Lucía said, and took the blanket that was on the sofa and started folding it meticulously. 'I'm sad. Why do we insist on leading lives that are not of our own choosing?'

'True. And *you* don't have a daughter,' I said.

She threw a cushion at me.

'No, I don't,' she half-smiled. 'Lucky my papá didn't live to see it. He would have been so disappointed.'

Lucía went quiet. Her gaze rested on the distance, as if she were watching a TV show on the wall. I thought about how many women felt they had spoiled their lives trying to please a third party, for doing things only to be seen doing them, rather than out of pleasure or purpose. Perhaps there were men who did the same, but I had no evidence of that.

While I didn't believe the same was the case for me, I knew I had left, almost fled, one society that felt too restricting, only to land in a country where I was always a foreigner. I was a bird with no tree and, yet, I was at ease. Even so, I wasn't completely happy. It was so difficult to know how to give of oneself in the perfect measure. To give oneself to others without losing oneself. I couldn't help smiling in irony, because those were the kinds of things Ramelli wrote about.

'There are so many women who don't ever come to realise what you're telling me,' I said.

'Well, what I wouldn't give to be one of them,' said Lucía.

I lit a cigarette, and Lucía stole a drag.

'I don't remember you smoking,' I said.

'I didn't use to, before you went to France – actually, I hated cigarettes,' she said, taking another drag. 'It's in the calendar, see' – she got up and turned the page to July – 'this red circle means that from that day forward no one smokes in here.'

'And we're smoking,' I said.

'Of course, we're the exception.'

'Sounds fair,' I replied.

'I've been wondering for a long time how so much money could come in from the book sales … I couldn't work it out, but maybe I looked the other way, didn't want to know.'

'You can't blame yourself.'

'Whom should we blame, then?'

'No one.'

'In this country, no one's to blame for anything.'

'Where are you going with this?'

'Someone has to take responsibility, Claire. Someone must be guilty.'

'So, you're going to be the one? You're volunteering?'

'Did you know there are more than 2,200 species of fleas?' said Lucía, draining her glass.

'Who could be capable of stealing money destined for health services?' I asked.

'My ex-husband!' said Lucía, pouring herself another glass. 'The man I slept beside for more than three decades!'

'Right, not you.'

'The guru of spirituality and everyday life values. The guy who preaches about good living and transparency in books that I write!'

'What was that, Lucía?'

'Which part?' she said with reddened eyes.

'Lucía. What on earth? Are you serious?'

She didn't say anything.

'You write the books? Are you telling me that Eduardo's books are really your own?'

Then she just smiled at me.

'Did you really write a book called *I Love Myself*?'

I laughed. Then my eyes were watering and my whole body was shaking. My reaction was as ferocious as it was unexpected. I fell back into the sofa. Lucía looked at me, surprised at first, then bit by bit she was infected with laughter, too, until it wore the two of us out. We grew calmer. Now was not the time to flood Lucía with uncomfortable questions like how she had ended up becoming her ex-husband's ghost writer. Making the confession was already big enough.

'Now you're on your feet, don't you think that below your shoe there might be a beautiful pair of fleas copulating?'

That got a smile out of me.

'You've dedicated your life to human beings when what really interested you were mites; how could you get so far away from yourself?'

'I got carried along.'

By midday we were both drunk. Lucía prepared a double espresso.

'And you haven't thought about trying to write novels?' I asked, a cup of coffee in my hands.

'I've never even considered it.'

'You could write a graphic novel about copulating fleas!' I teased. 'You've certainly got enough imagination.'

'It's a serious interest, Claire,' she said. 'Anyway, you're the one with the novelistic streak. Maybe this very moment you're working on something and you don't even know it.'

'I'm a little old for that,' I said.

'Aren't you always insisting that at this age we're at our peak?'

'Well, for some things. But for others … Guess who's coming to see me in an hour.'

'Who?'

'Your ex-husband's associate.'

'Diazgranados?'

'The very same.'

'That's odd.'

'I know.'

'A Muslim is more likely to believe in Baby Jesus than that guy is to believe in psychoanalysis.'

'I don't see why a Muslim has no right to believe in Baby Jesus,' I said.

'The point is, if those two have done what everyone says they've done, they're dangerous.'

'Those two?'

'I doubt Eduardo is innocent.'

'Do you think they're capable of killing someone?' I asked, feeling suddenly sober.

'I don't know. This is no joke,' said Lucía. 'They've stolen money through writs, in the name of dead patients, through medications and supplies that were never delivered … Here everyone's entangled. It's a mess. *La Recontra* reported three billion stolen. Go on, go to your appointment,' added Lucía. 'Thank you for coming over. And don't call my phone if you want to tell me about any of it. I'm not joking.'

'So let's meet up next week. Want to come to mine? That way I'll be able to tell you what Diazgranados was after, and we'll work out what you're going to do.'

'It's going to be a nightmare. No one will believe I didn't know anything,' said Lucía.

'People might phone to ask you to tell them about it, but then everything will go quiet, you'll see. But can I ask you something?'

'Whatever you want.'

'How did you fall in love with Eduardo? I don't understand it.'

'I don't, either. I felt fondly towards him. He seemed helpless to me, I liked to feel I could be a comfort to him … I don't know.'

We gave each other a long hug at the door.

'Do you remember the Karen I told you about? A client of hers died in strange circumstances after a date with Luis Armando Diazgranados, Aníbal's son. She's been called to testify,' I said.

'And what do you think? That his boy was involved in her death?'

'Honestly, I don't know,' I said. 'But maybe they're more dangerous than we imagine.'

'I know. I doubt Eduardo understands how deep he's in,' said Lucía.

'Do you think he's innocent?'

'Innocent, no. Even so: he might be a white-collar criminal, but he's no murderer,' she added.

'Then you should warn him,' I said. 'He might be more naive than you think. Maybe he doesn't realise the danger he's in.'

'Why? Do you think they could do something to him?'

'I don't know,' I said.

'They're associates, but Eduardo is getting all the blame for this,' said Lucía.

'Exactly. Diazgranados might worry that Eduardo could get him in hot water. Don't you think?'

'Don't leave me alone in this.'

We gave each other another hug and I left.

31.

Karen wasn't one to look back. She was so absorbed in her day-to-day that she didn't stop to remember. Yet every now and then, some part of her old self assailed her, even if only for a moment. At a client's house in the Santa Ana neighbourhood, she stroked a curtain, thinking about the dress she could have made with its fabric. Every now and again, an idea, an image, a smell reminded her who she was. But who was she? On looking at herself in the mirror, ready to step out – her hair straightened, and wearing high boots, a handbag and a trench coat – she knew this Karen could walk into any building without being searched, that they would call her 'Señorita' or 'Señora', a certain respect in their tone of voice, and that this would be a response to her outfit, her silky hair and her way of modulating her words. Karen wanted to be the woman she saw in the mirror as she left the apartment with its marble floor and golden taps, not the woman who stroked a curtain and imagined a dress made from its fabric. And not the woman who was nostalgic for the sticky heat of Cartagena at midday, for the salsa dive where the walls sweated and she surrendered to a man's body just to become one with the music, with no need to say a word, free to go and sit at her table as soon as the song finished. Despite her hunger, fear, lack of sleep and constant state of alert, Karen still wanted to be the scarred person she saw in the mirror; broken, but respectable.

Perhaps because of this – because she poured so much effort into being a woman of rich and educated appearance, because she yearned to be truly the image she projected – Karen was loving strolling through the Andino Mall one Sunday morning, amid expensive display cases, mothers racing to buy a birthday present for a friend's daughter at the last minute, chubby kids getting on the indoor amusement-park rides over and over again, older people going into the cinema for the discounted senior-citizen session, businessmen searching for an anniversary or birthday gift. Looking rich was enough to make Karen feel welcomed by those who had rejected her previously.

Perhaps that's why Doña Josefina de Brigard's comment took her by surprise. She asked about the lipstick she'd started wearing the past few weeks. Naively, Karen responded enthusiastically. Then she asked where Karen had bought her coat, boots and handbag. Finally she said:

'You can't make a silk purse out of a sow's ear.'

In response to Karen's shocked, offended expression, she continued.

'None of it goes together, honey. You look like a jumble of all the women who pass through your cubicle.'

Karen didn't say anything for a moment.

'May I excuse myself, Señora?'

'You may,' said Josefina de Brigard, fixing her eyes on some papers, not looking up at her again.

Karen shut herself in the lavatory once more, but this time, instead of crying or cutting herself or calling Wílmer or me, she scrutinised herself for a long time in the mirror, trying to understand where she had gone wrong.

32.

I got home ten minutes late. Aníbal Diazgranados opened my door and motioned for me to follow him.

'Claire, my dear, welcome.'

He invited me through to the little room where I conduct my therapy sessions and took my place, so that I had no option but to sit in the patient's spot. I wondered where Luz, the maid, could be, but didn't dare ask.

'Luz has ducked out to the pharmacy to get me my blood-pressure pills.' He had read my thoughts.

'She agreed to leave you here alone?'

'Let's just say I can be persuasive.'

'Through threats?' I asked.

'Through being empathic,' he winked.

'And how does one learn that kind of empathy?'

'Why don't you tell me, Doctor Claire? Are you the kind of person to mistreat the maids? My wife does – and she's a good woman, don't get me wrong. To this day, I've never met a good woman who doesn't.'

'What are you saying?'

'Is this how you earn 300,000 pesos per hour? Answering questions with counter-questions?'

'Is it so difficult for you, Minister, to earn your wage?'

197

'Let's say it's more difficult than lying on a couch asking silly questions.'

'Is that how you see my occupation?'

'Your questioning style reveals a certain aggressiveness, Doctor,' said Diazgranados.

His mole eyes shone, tiny in his large and flabby face, offset by a voluminous double chin.

'Can I offer you a glass of water?'

'Yes please,' said Aníbal.

I went out to fetch one. I wondered how he got Luz to leave the apartment. I came back with the glass and found him loosening the knot in his tie, as if he were short on air. I desperately wanted to throw him out of my apartment, but I contained myself. Then I wanted to throw the water in his face, but I didn't. I'm a coward. I passed him the glass of water, which he drank in long gulps while I thought about how to do away with him right there, in my consulting room. Perhaps with the wrought-iron candelabra, I said to myself, or with the letter opener inherited from my grandmother. The manatee man made noises as he drank. His hands were thick and hairy, with small fingers. Now I wondered how he got in – not only into the apartment, but into the building. Luz has strict instructions, as all maids do, and so does the security guard. He isn't allowed to let in anyone without authorisation from the owner or tenant of the property.

'Why did you make an appointment?'

'I saw you talking to my wife at the minister's daughter's wedding.'

'I don't understand.'

'You said hello to Rosario, my wife.'

'We go to the same beauty salon. Is that a crime?'

'Why, is someone talking about a crime, here?'

I felt suddenly suffocated by the faint drunkenness that was not letting me think, by my fear and the excessive aftershave in the air. What must he smell like when he doesn't pour half a bottle of patchouli on himself each morning? Nausea churned in my stomach.

'Imagine: my grandfather was a dedicated conservative. He would tell me how he used to swing machetes during La Violencia. He used to train fishermen to cut off heads like plucking the petals off daisies. Did you know a head can keep screaming after it's been lopped off?'

'I didn't, but it seems scientifically improbable.'

'And you don't find it funny?' said Diazgranados. He cackled.

'Honestly, no.'

'Look, Doctor, I was brought up in a tough family. We've always been involved in politics; we've defended our own with our teeth, like wolves.'

'I still don't understand what all this is about.'

'It's simple: you give what you get. Reap what you sow. Understood?' said Aníbal.

'Are you threatening me?'

'You've got a fixation on that little word, Doctor. You might need to psychoanalyse that.'

'Our time is up,' I said, looking at the clock while Aníbal pulled out a wad of notes.

'I can buy your time. A week, a month, a year. Your entire life.'

'That's not how it works,' I said.

'I get it. You're just like all intellectuals and academics. You stick to the rules and regulations, but ignore reality. Doctor, allow me to tell you something loud and clear: you're the one refusing to see the way the world works.'

'And what's the reality I'm ignoring, according to you?'

'The reality that a head screams after it's been lopped off.'

'Another threat.'

'Call it what you will. I'm just saying that there are things better left untested. Take it as advice from a friend.'

'I thank you for it,' I said. 'Now leave.'

'Is it true that what is said in here stays here? If it were any different, your professionalism would be called into question.'

I didn't manage to respond. I was trembling. It was an effort to get out of the couch and open the door for him.

'Please,' I said.

Before getting up, he said: 'That little friend of yours, Karen Valdés, she's of no consequence, but I see you've got that coloniser I've-come-to-save-the-poor attitude. A word of advice, Doctor: let the girl accept her fate.

We've got her case sorted; there's nothing more to be done; whoever interferes will get burnt.'

'What did Karen do?'

'Karen is not what you think she is, Doctor. Karen Valdés is a prostitute and a criminal.'

'That's a lie. What are you going to do to her?' I asked, my voice breaking.

'Señora Dalvard, calm down, be grateful that you and your daughter are enjoying freedom and good health. And now, you will understand that, for a minister of the Republic, being absent from the plenary session has disastrous consequences for the fatherland. We're debating projects of enormous magnitude, such as health reform, for example, and nothing less than the legal framework for the peace process. That's why I ask, Señora, that you don't give me reason to come back here. For your own good, for mine and for the fatherland. One last thing before I go: do you know what medicine I should take to slim down?'

'No,' I said.

'Of course. Just as I thought. Your "medical" training is only good for grappling with imaginary illnesses.'

He got up unhurriedly from my chair, and on opening the door I saw Luz in the doorway of the kitchen, timidly clutching a package.

'Thank you, sister,' Aníbal said with a small bow.

'Thank you, brother. It was a pleasure to be of assistance.'

'How did he get in?' I asked Luz as soon as the door closed.

'He's the pastor. Politician and pastor.'

'He said that and got through?'

'Yes, Señora.'

'Why?'

'He's a brother at my congregation.'

A bout of retching made me run towards the bathroom, where I threw up the whiskies I'd drunk with Lucía. It was barely two o'clock. I had four patients to go before the end of the day. After gargling, I smoothed my skirt in front of the mirror, brushed a lock of hair behind my ear and went back to my consulting room, this time taking a seat on the leather chair.

The afternoon went by slowly. I listened to my patients as if I were inside a fish tank, their voices far off and distorted. When the last session finally ended, I went for a lie down and watched the news bulletin. Between images of the cold spell, of people stuck in mud with no roof over their heads or food, I found myself thinking about my relationship with Luz, built on a series of rituals learned from childhood. She had learned the bowed head – the 'Yes, Señora', 'No, Señora', 'What time would you like to have lunch, Doña Claire?' – and I had learned to give instructions, head held high, voice terse as a bowstring: 'The chicken was delicious', 'You can go home now', 'Don't forget to vacuum the consulting room.' And Luz, head bowed, taught to nod, only smiled.

Smiled and nodded. I felt a bit embarrassed that Aníbal could connect with her on a human level in a matter of seconds, when I'd seen her every day over the past year and a half. What did I know about Luz? That she was from Cómbita, that she had a son and two grandchildren. Nothing else. I didn't even know if she took her coffee with sugar.

33.

Karen had been raped, and her therapy had been to fall to pieces. In time this breaking apart had made her more resistant. Obedience was, in her, a form of self-destruction.

There was a crack in the wall. She thought about telling Eduardo, but contained herself. He stroked her face with tenderness, his eyes glazed. To Karen, he looked older than ever.

'I really like you,' he said, caressing her shoulder.

It was 29 October, two days before Lucía's birthday, Halloween, and Eduardo's appearance in the tabloids as the man responsible for rerouting close to a billion pesos of the more than three billion stolen from the nation's health sector.

'I have a favour to ask,' he said.

'What is it?' asked Karen, impatient to get in the shower.

'Could you help me out by holding on to some money for me? It would be two weeks, tops.'

Karen didn't answer.

'If it makes you more comfortable, I'll tell you the story, just so you know how much I trust you and that I wouldn't hurt you.'

'What story?'

Eduardo told her about the early hours of 23 July, when, lying on the sofa at his ex-wife's after drinking too many whiskies, he got a call from someone close to him who wanted him to cover up the death of a young woman.

He told her about the encounter in the 24-hour Carulla supermarket, the morning they decided to cover up the death. He told her about the doctor involved, and the taxi driver, both of whom she had spoken to personally. Karen looked at him as if seeing him for the first time. It seemed impossible that the same man who had covered up a crime could be the author of the books she read. She felt disenchanted and at the same time trapped in her own story.

Karen supposed that the dangerous associate was Aníbal Diazgranados, Luis Armando's father. At the end, as if talking about someone who had nothing to do with the events just recounted, Eduardo added: 'If one day something happens, Aníbal Diazgranados, the minister, is a friend. Go to him. He knows you have the money.'

'I still haven't said I'll safeguard it for him,' thought Karen, but didn't say so. Instead, she asked, 'Would this have anything to do with Luis Armando Diazgranados?'

'He's Aníbal's son,' said Eduardo. 'Has he been a client of yours?'

'No,' said Karen. And although the question offended her, she didn't say any more.

'Well, that doesn't surprise me. Rumour has it he's a faggot,' said Eduardo, wrapping himself in a silk dressing gown.

In the shower, questions ran through Karen's head. Could Sabrina have been meeting up with a different Luis Armando Diazgranados? She wondered what would happen if she didn't agree to safeguard Eduardo's money. When she got out, she heard voices in the living room. As she quickly got dressed, she decided to tell me everything. Standing next to a large suitcase, two men were looking at her. For the first time, she understood that she could be in danger.

'Karen, darling, they're going with you, to hide the money in your apartment.'

It was a large case, enough to hold around seventy kilos. One of the men had the nerve to look her up and down. He was armed.

'Your mission is simple, you put this in a safe place and wait until one of these gentlemen, if not me, comes to get it.'

Karen says she shot Eduardo a pleading look, to no avail.

He winked at her and smiled. 'Go with them, Piccolina, you'll be fine.'

34.

Before they would know if the note found in Sabrina's room was written by Luis Armando Diazgranados, they had to wait a few more days for the handwriting analysis results. As for everything else, they needed an order from the Prosecutor's Office to access the medical record at San Blas and, if the handwriting results confirmed a match, they could submit a request to interrogate Luis Armando Diazgranados and trace his calls.

Jorge Guzmán hadn't stopped pacing the living room of his ex-wife's apartment where they were gathered. His eyes were bloodshot. Consuelo Paredes was wringing her hands and murmuring to herself. Her brow was furrowed and she didn't seem to be following the conversation.

'Cojack, tell me you'll manage it.'

'Manage what, Doctor Guzmán?'

'To catch the murderer.'

'I'll do everything within my power.'

Consuelo poured a herbal tea for her ex-husband.

'Oh, hun,' she said to him. 'We would have been better off not knowing his name; we would be much more at peace.'

'There's more,' interrupted Cojack. 'I think I have our taxi driver. I was talking to some friends in intelligence and I've got it down to three candidates: they all operate in the area and sometimes do jobs on the side.'

'You mean they're hitmen?'

'They call themselves hands for hire.'

'And you've located all three of them?' asks Guzmán.

'I know of one because he's involved with really big fish. On Thursdays, he plays billiards at a bar in Chapinero.'

'So tomorrow,' said Guzmán.

'That's right. Tomorrow I'll pay him a little visit. I'll have news for you as soon as I've spoken to him.'

'And what about the doctor?' asked Consuelo.

'The doctor won't talk.'

'What if we make him?' asked Guzmán.

Consuelo glanced at her ex-husband in surprise.

'I don't offer those kinds of services, but I can get you someone, if you want,' said Cojack.

Jorge Guzmán went quiet, but the fury on his face radiated throughout the room like a migraine.

35.

I called Lucía and told her, word for word, what Aníbal Diazgranados had said. I was scared.

'You can't be serious, Claire,' she said.

'What if he hurts Eduardo? Your ex is a very silly bad guy,' I said.

'I'll call him right away,' said Lucía.

An hour later I called her again. 'Have you spoken to Eduardo?'

'He didn't answer, must be playing golf.'

'Will you let me know?'

'As soon as I speak to him.'

If either of us had believed Eduardo was in real danger, we might have acted differently, might have headed out to find him. Lucía left messages on his phone. First saying: 'Call me when you can, please,' and then: 'Eduardo, it's about Diazgranados, answer me, I'm begging you.' When he finally answered, he was in the car on his way to meeting up with Doctor Venegas.

'Eduardo, do you realise Aníbal went to Claire's today and threatened her?' she said finally.

'What are you talking about?'

'He threatened to kill her.'

'What do you mean?' he said, and laughed. 'You know what, woman? It's Halloween. I know that ghost stories are more likely to get to us at this time of year, but relax, drink a chai, wrap up warm …'

'Can you be serious for once in your life?'

'I'm being serious, completely serious … If you give me fifteen minutes, I'm just parking. I won't be long, I'll call you back.'

'Eduardo, be careful, okay?'

'Is it the telenovelas you watch at night?'

'I don't watch telenovelas, I watch dramas.'

'Well, that trash is damaging your pretty head, turn off the TV.'

'You sound content,' said Lucía.

'A young woman has been coming over to warm up my bed.'

'What a surprise.'

'You're such a drag. I'll call you back. And by the way, happy birthday, gorgeous.'

'I thought you'd forgotten.'

'How could I, when today's a special day for all of humanity?' said Eduardo.

'Are you saying that because of the article in *La Recontra*, the one about you embezzling state funds?'

'Shut up, woman, that's why I'm not answering my phone!' he said. Then he hung up.

Two hours before, he had been lying on his sofa, his shirt open and pants down. Despite the scandal, he was happy. Having that suitcase safe calmed him. In the worst-case scenario, he would be put under house arrest for a few years and then he'd be safe, he and his money. It would all be worth it in the long run.

His chest was covered in white hairs. He was in good shape, and Karen saw he was relaxed. His eyes closed, he let her do her thing. Soon everything would go back to normal. He stroked Karen's hair, and now she tried to smile.

'What would you do with all that money, if it were yours?' he asked, still caressing her. She shrugged her shoulders.

'I'd end up in trouble,' she said with a half-smile.

'But what would you like to do?'

'I'd like to go far away.'

'You could go far away and do other things, too, it's a lot of money.'

'I've always wanted to do it in a pool, you know?' said Karen, suddenly standing up, evasive. 'Have you ever?'

'It's nothing special,' said Ramelli. 'But if you want, we can do it in a pool now, so you're not left wondering.'

Karen smiled.

'Or would you prefer to go to a Halloween party?' he asked.

'I hate dressing up,' said Karen. She took his hand. 'Come on. Let's go.'

She was moved that, at almost seventy years of age, Eduardo let her lead him to the pool so she could fulfil her adolescent fantasy. Until then, she had only ever been in pools crammed with other people.

They came out of the lift, removed their dressing gowns, got into the heated water. Through the glass, they could see the city lights scattering to the west.

'What's this, what you and I have?' Eduardo said after a long kiss.

'I'm the one safekeeping your suitcase,' said Karen, and let out a yelp when a middle-aged woman came in, looked at them sidelong, left her robe on one of the pool chairs and slipped into the water.

'Today's not our lucky day,' said Karen, adjusting her bra.

'Would you believe me if I said that in more than a year of living here, I've never had to share the pool with anyone?'

Before getting out, Eduardo took her by the waist. 'I like you a lot,' he said, gazing into her eyes.

Karen burst out laughing.

'You're so insensitive,' said Eduardo.

'I'm sorry,' added Karen, still laughing.

Eduardo took her arm and pulled her to his chest.

'I'm going to fuck you until your head explodes.'

Karen kept quiet. She got out of the pool in silence. She dried herself with the towel while she watched the woman with thick, pale legs doing backstroke.

'It's late,' she said, suddenly anxious.

'It's almost eight.'

'Exactly, it's late.'

'Come up for a bit.'

'It's been a long day, I'd like to go home,' she said.

'Of course, you've got to go and count the money in the suitcase, if you didn't count it yesterday.'

Barefooted, they both got into the lift. The glass box carried them skywards, views of Bogotá all around them. Karen felt distant, disconnected. She was overcome by dizziness, then her mouth went dry. She felt a pain in her chest. She was hyperventilating. She'd gone days without feeling this way. Eduardo stared at her cut ankles, then at her wrists, seemed to be noticing them only now. The doors of the lift opened. Karen's hands were sweating. He helped her into the apartment, laid her down on the bed and went to the kitchen to fetch a glass of water. Karen was still not breathing normally. He called Doctor Venegas and asked him what to do.

'Do I need a prescription for that?' Karen heard Eduardo ask.

'I'm feeling better now,' she said, though her heart was still racing.

It wasn't yet 9 p.m. when he decided to go to Doctor Venegas's place. The doctor would give him something for Karen. He took the car.

'I'll be right back, don't move.'

Karen turned on the TV and stared at it for about half an hour. She was hardly taking anything in, until to her shock an old photo of Eduardo came on screen.

Everything points to the well-known self-help author as the person behind this cover-up. He is also president of Health Cross, responsible for operating San Blas Hospital in Bogotá ...

Karen called to tell him what she was seeing on the news, but he didn't answer. The fourth time she called, a police officer answered and asked what her relationship was to the deceased.

'To the what, Officer?' said Karen, sitting up.

'To the dead man, Señorita. I'm sorry to be giving you the news like this, but the owner of the phone you're calling was found shot dead on the corner of Calle 76 and Carrera 5, along with another victim identified as Roberto Venegas, a surgeon from San Blas Hospital.'

It was a little after 10 p.m. The official continued speaking, but Karen had stopped listening.

36.

It was the second time in four months that she'd gone to a funeral. She felt like her whole life could be summed up in that period. She dressed as well as she could, despite her despondency. She put the little energy she had into doing her hair up in a high bun, painting her lips an earthy colour, and choosing appropriate footwear, a blouse with a moderate neckline, the Massimo Dutti trench coat and the small black Carolina Herrera handbag that Eduardo had given her, which she was yet to use. She had seen him for the first time at Sabrina Guzmán's funeral. Perhaps, if she'd been alert to the signs, she would have understood that no good can come from a relationship with a man you meet at a funeral. This time, as she went into the Church of the Immaculate Conception, she felt she was a different person. People were crowded inside. Karen chose the final pew, and sat down closest to the wall. There were men in suits, bodyguards, armoured SUVs at the church entrance, tinted windows, a few children, some young people, a lot of fans of Eduardo. National radio and TV crews were there. They wanted to talk to Lucía, who didn't seem interested in making statements to the press.

It was a farewell for 'Colombia's great spiritual guide to emotional lost causes', as one journalist described him. Karen didn't take in the priest's words. Nor did she hear when a soldier in uniform repeated the word 'love' three times as he raised a fist in the air. The cough of an old man echoed throughout the church. The choir was out of tune. Everything seemed wrong, off-key.

Maybe the general dissonance was due to the foul way Ramelli had been killed. He was an elegant man, or at least someone who made the effort to be. Yet he had been caught wearing a sweatshirt, shot at point blank on a street corner in the exclusive Rosales neighbourhood, and left to die like a dog until a good Samaritan called the police. It was all a big misunderstanding.

When the soldier finished, a woman with acid burns on her face got up, grabbed the microphone and said that Eduardo had taught her to survive, that thanks to him she hadn't put a bullet in her head. A few people applauded timidly. Diazgranados's wife cried inconsolably. Karen realised that his wife was her client, Rosario Trujillo. She was finding it hard to breathe.

She would tell me later that while all this was happening, she felt seared as if by the midday Cartagena heat. It took her back to being squashed into a bus while the fare collector announced the stops: 'María Auxiliadora', 'Castellana', 'Blas de Lezo'. She was carried along by the smells – loquats, sea bream – under a sun that blurred the borders of everything, so that it was all gilded in a golden haze, sweet like coconut, or like mandarin juice. One man was selling posies for a thousand pesos to the young man next to him, and another was selling English–Spanish school dictionaries. An elderly woman was saying to her grandson that she wasn't about to pay two thousand pesos for a dictionary, as he looked over the pencils being sold by another black man who had also hopped on the big old bus, which was like a whale out of its element, with fewer passengers than street sellers – one had highlighters, another had Bristol almanacs, others had fresh water, coconut water, key rings, phone covers, stickers, magazines, scapulars, biscuits. When Karen wanted to get off, the fare collector shouted out the bus stops once more beneath the suffocating heat that made grime collect under fingernails and wouldn't let you breathe. And that same heat was felt by those riding the next bus along, which was headed for the same place, almost empty too. All the buses had six, seven, eight passengers and were run-down, begging for more passengers with the image of Our Lady of Mount Carmel, of The Blessed Child, of Our Lady of Guadalupe, of Jesus Christ. And the buses that had signs saying CHRIST LIVES cut in front of those brandishing Our Lady of Mount Carmel, because they all had to get there first, but there was only one road, and there were roadworks, plus there was only one lane because the other was closed – that was where they put the bus station, though now it was abandoned and its windows were broken and it was full of debris. If you walked through the Bazurto market, the stalls would say: GOD PROTECTS THIS SHOP, BLOOD OF CHRIST JUICES and GO WITH GOD FRESH CUTS. There was an overpowering smell of death, of guts, of pork, fish and tripe, of entrails splashed on the floor, of cow and pig carcasses where the black men who cleaned the animal guts walked barefooted. A cart went by called LITTLE KAREN, and she wondered how she would feel if she had a father who worked in the market or wherever and called his cart LITTLE KAREN, if she had a father who knew how to make egg *arepas*, yuca pastries, or nice and fresh *peto* with lots of cinnamon. Now in Cartagena it was all white buildings with blue windows, all of it, all of it, said her mamá, as if there were no green, yellow, red or transparent glass, and A-huh, said her mamá, and A-huh, said Karen, so many buses, all off to the same destinations, and that searing heat during the wait, and the smell of sea dirt, of sea sweat, of sea water, and the constant pulse of *champeta* music, *champeta* at la Boquilla beach, in a club in El Bosque neighbourhood, and hearing the neighbourhood's *picó* sound systems boom, taking a siesta in the rocking chair, and mamá preparing tamarind balls in the doorway of the house, oh to hear her say, 'Child, don't look for me because if you do you'll find me,' because no one called her child any more, and no one looked for her, much less found her. Even she couldn't find herself, and she didn't know where she was gone, she was getting more lost all the time, more here and there at the same time and yet nowhere at once. Here no one played cards in the shade of a mango tree, there was no calabash tree here, no Pentecostal church with the mango tree out front, no park, no New Christ the Redeemer Church, no street sellers offering corn *bollos*, there was nothing here, thought Karen, no Emiliano, no mamá, here there were only irritable people, and death prowling beneath a lead sky, and she felt the searing heat and started to sweat because in her mouth there was the taste of tamarind, not dried tamarind but those sweet little tamarind balls her grandmother used to make, back when she was a little girl, back when she still had a grandmother. Back when she wanted to be a beauty queen, before *champeta* music and her first communion, before thinking about sex and knowing it was a sin until she was married, before going to Mass at the neighbourhood church, before crossing herself whenever she passed by any church, no matter its denomination, before being top of her class, before wanting to be a beautician, if she ever did want that, before the fever overcame her body to the heat of *champeta*, before messing around with a black man old enough to be her father, before getting pregnant, before becoming who she was, before understanding she couldn't escape herself, that this – this body like a palm tree, like a gazelle, this frightened face, this listless sadness, this pride that had failed to find a foothold in this world, this drive to get somewhere that had nowhere to go – this was who she was. She was another bird with no tree, in a cement city where there were no corner shops, no slot machines, no old quarter behind walls where Monaco royalty and Hollywood actors took their holidays, that walled city where she would never belong, since it was only for tourists and the few rich families left. Here there were no classical music concerts in the street, no horse and carriage carrying a pair of Canadian sweethearts, no pig wandering around a patio like it was no big deal, or wet clothes hung along the fences to dry in the wind, just as there were no fences, fences to protect oneself from the outside when locked inside, nor roofs with shards of glass cemented into them to deter thieves, no guard dog to do the same, though 'if you give fish to a dog that's not from the tropics, it will get mangy,' said her mamá, as if she'd had a cold-weather dog, as if she'd been in a cold-weather place, as if she knew anything about dogs. Karen realised that she was one of those animals from the tropics; she wondered again what she was doing here in this icebox, what brought her to Bogotá, to learn the slow and smooth-tongued way of speaking, to smile, to fake friendliness, to eat *almojábana* buns instead of yuca pastries, to forget who she was. Her Emiliano was now farther away than ever, her Emi who said that no one knew how to massage his feet like his mamita, because he called her 'mamita' and, when he was being especially affectionate, 'mamitica', and Karen – who hadn't touched his feet in almost a year, a quarter of his life, as said her own mamá, a quarter of your son's life you haven't been here, young lady – Karen, wrapped up in her thoughts, looked at the church doors, where a group of people had remained outside clutching signs that read MASTER OF ALL MASTERS, YOU'LL NEVER DIE and SAVE ME A PLACE IN HEAVEN to say farewell to Ramelli. Karen looked at them as if she weren't really there, remembered Ramelli was dead, and once more there was the nausea, and the bus shuffling along Pedro de Heredia, and her mamá saying 'the dark-skinned women selling fruit on the beach', as if she weren't dark skinned, too, and what was her fear of saying black, anyhow. People were leaving and the rain was gaining momentum and the SUVs parked along the avenue were tearing off. Karen stayed seated, observing without being seen, and she was sweating, all sticky, and there was the smell of tamarind, but once more she was in the rain, always the rain and the exhaust fumes in this grey city, and the grey dust, the grey clouds, the grey clothing of office workers, the grey smog, the fucking *greyness* of this city was going to make her die of damned sadness, and if she had a father, she would say *Is it greyness or greyity?* If she had a father, he would know the answer, and if he didn't know, what the hell, she would have a father and wouldn't feel like she was dying, or that she was already dead, a ghost wandering the streets, that's why people stepped on her, that's why they elbowed her and trod on her in the Transmilenio bus, because they didn't see her. Eduardo had seen her, Eduardo had caressed her and therefore had seen her, and he had paid her and they had fucked like living beings do, but now he was dead. She stuck out her tongue, tasted the rough air. The heavy, toxic air. The rain drops like needles. She got on a bus, hung on to the metal rail, smelled once more the concentrated sweat. Perhaps she was alive, after all. She was alive because in here it smelled like shit. She was alive because more than forty-seven guys had fucked her in the past sixteen weeks. She was alive because a revolting and embittered fat man had raped her. She was alive, just not for the right reasons.

37.

Cojack's call left Consuelo short of breath. She called Jorge first and told him to come over; it was urgent.

'I'm in Abastos.'

'Okay, but come, as fast as you can.'

'As soon as I can,' he said and hung up.

While she waited, her hands trembling, Consuelo opened her planner and called the lawyer, who didn't answer. Then she called the National Society of Psychoanalysts, and was given my telephone number. She dialled right away and when I didn't answer, left a message: 'I'm calling on behalf of Karen Valdés. I'm Sabrina Guzmán's mother. Call me back, please,' and left her number. She called the lawyer again.

'I'm going to have to step down from the case,' he told her.

'What? Just when it's getting off its feet?'

'Yes, forgive me.'

'But what happened?'

'A matter of a *force majeure*, Señora Consuelo.'

'Don't give me that,' said Consuelo, her voice breaking.

'This morning a small coffin arrived at my house. Inside were the names of my son and daughter. Please understand,' he said, and hung up.

Consuelo tried his number again but it was useless.

She searched for the forensics officer's number. She'd spoken to him on two previous occasions.

'Señora Consuelo, I was just thinking about you, I wanted to tell you that someone's been hacking your daughter's Facebook page. But that's as far as I got, because I've just been informed that another prosecutor has been assigned the case. That means he will put together another team, and I will probably be reassigned.'

'But why? No one has said anything to me ...'

'Whatever they tell you will be a lie, Señora. I've got to go, I'm being called.'

'Why are they doing this?'

'It's possible they're trying to shift blame for the crime to an innocent, to draw attention away from the true culprit. Forgive me, Señora, but I've got to hang up.'

Consuelo stayed like that, telephone pressed to her ear, bewildered.

38.

She stepped inside House of Beauty, leaving a puddle of rainwater in the entrance. Annie on reception looked on insolently as Karen shut herself in the toilets. She crossed her fingers, hoping for a hectic afternoon, even though it was Tuesday, so she wouldn't have to put up with her colleagues' conversations. She missed Susana. She cried, the hand dryer masking her sobs, before heading out into a clique of women who she found duller and more aged each day.

She acted like an automaton. Panic overcame her at different moments. The urge to hurt herself was overwhelming. She was hounded by a constant image of cutting one of her calves with a scalpel to the point of slicing off a piece of muscle. She imagined mutilating a finger, an ear. Later, when she checked, she found a wound on her ankle, another on her elbow. She didn't remember doing that to herself.

Karen was going up the stairs when the unmistakable, nasal voice of Karen Ardila interrupted her:

'Pocahontas, is that you?' she laughed.

She kept on going. Yet she hadn't even shut the cubicle door when Annie called to tell her Doña Karen was on her way.

Karen Ardila got undressed, letting her clothes fall to the floor. Her jacket and handbag were the only things she handed over. Karen felt irritated, but wanted to avoid a confrontation.

'What would you like today?' she asked, collecting her thong, bra, blouse and shoes from the floor.

'A full Brazilian.'

'Just a moment, Doña Karen. I'll heat the wax.'

She moved fast. She cut the strips of cloth, decided to forgo the electric blanket so they'd get through it quickly, for the good of them both. The nakedness of that body, which she had to turn from one side to another – its impurities, the mole on the hip, the scant hair on the pubis, the birth mark near the vagina, the dampness – it all nauseated her.

She looked at the pussy in front of her: red, damp, open right in front of her nose, like a threat, like an insult that smelled of rotten fish, because that's what it smelled like, that's what she was smelling. Doña Karen called her by name:

'Karen? Are you feeling all right? You're sweating.'

Karen would have liked to respond – she was grateful Doña Karen had used her name, it was the first time – but by then it was too late, out of the corner of her eye she had seen her frizzing hair in the mirror and she was angry. All that effort. She retched so hard she couldn't answer Doña Karen, and she had no choice but to leave the cubicle, disobeying House of Beauty rules, praying she'd reach the toilet in time. Once there she threw up, feeling a great ball of disgust in her stomach.

Karen splashed water on her face. She got a razor blade out of her pocket. She made a cut on her forearm. A faint buzz ran through her body. She repeated the operation three, four, seven times. They were superficial cuts. She wanted to make a deeper one. She bled. She opened the first-aid kit, put a plaster on herself. She lowered her socks and made a deeper cut on her ankle. She let out a deep breath of air. She put on another plaster. She wrapped the blade in toilet paper, there was a lot of blood, it stained the white socks of her uniform and her shoes, which were also white. She turned on the tap and wet her hair in fury, trying to straighten it. It was useless. It got wetter and frizzier. Karen was shouting. She was shut in the House of Beauty lavatory, tying to straighten her hair with water, and shouting. She took off her socks and rinsed them in the basin. When she finished washing them, and was about to put them back on even though they were wet, she saw there was blood on the floor and crouched down to mop it up with a sock. She heard two knocks on the door, then footsteps, then the voice of Doña Josefina, and more movement and people coming and going. Karen sang and cleaned the floor with her sock, but the cut kept bleeding, as did the one on her forearm.

'Karen, open the door.'

It was Doña Josefina's voice. She didn't remember much more. When she opened her eyes, she was in her cubicle, the woman had gone. Around her ankle was a bandage, and there was cloth wrapped around her forearm and wrists. A few minutes later, Doña Josefina appeared in the cubicle doorway.

'Come up to my office, when you're feeling up to it.'

Karen closed her eyes and sank into a deep sleep.

39.

Josefina de Brigard asked Karen to leave House of Beauty immediately. She recommended she seek psychological help.

'Honey, you're sick. You can't be here. It would be best if someone came to pick you up.'

Karen tried Susana's number, but she didn't answer. Then she called me, and caught me when I was having a coffee with Lucía. I said I'd go get her right away. Lucía came with me. We helped her pack her things. Karen insisted on seeing Susana, so I promised to help locate her.

We came to my apartment. For the first time, she came into my consulting room. We laid her down on the couch. Lucía passed her an alpaca blanket, and she covered her feet with it. The afternoon was deepening. A cold day, like almost all days here.

'You were right, she's beautiful,' said Lucía.

Karen dropped off to sleep. Sunlight fell on her face, leaving one side bright and the other in shadow. I made a pot of tea. We turned on the fountain on the terrace, just outside the consulting-room window. The sound of water always helps calm my thoughts. I hoped it would have the same effect on Karen. Lucía started reading a psychiatry magazine that was at hand.

'I'd like to open my own consulting room. Think I'm too old for that?'

'You'd be very good,' I said.

We watched over her as she slept for almost an hour. When she opened her eyes, it was night.

'You're Lucía,' she said finally.

'That's right,' Lucía said with a smile.

Lucía was a woman who inspired trust. She had a placid face. Serene. And her smile was sincere. Yet Karen didn't see that. She focused on her grey hair, her crow's feet, her yellowed teeth. She closed her eyes again.

'Would you like to sleep here?' I asked.

'Why are you doing this for me?'

'Because we want to,' Lucía hurried to respond. 'You're unwell.'

Karen opened her eyes again and stared at her.

'What do you want with me?' said Karen.

'I'd like to tell your story. In fact, both Claire and I would like to tell it.'

'How about I make pasta? Anyone hungry?' I asked.

'Not me,' said Karen.

I went to the kitchen and put spaghetti in a pan, then got tomato sauce out of the freezer and put it in a pan, too. I didn't leave them for long. Once the food was ready, I went to call them. Before knocking on the door, I heard them laughing. At the table, Karen drank the glass of wine as if it were water and asked for more. She did the same with the second and then asked for water before speaking.

'I'm going to do it,' she said finally.

'What?' I said.

'Tell you my story.'

'That deserves a toast.'

Karen had two helpings of pasta, and said she would take a sleeping pill when we dropped her home. It was important she had a restorative sleep. She said she'd taken some of the pills I'd given her. She was sleeping well. From now on, I'd oversee her medication, as well as her psychotherapy. We took her to her apartment. We agreed to meet up the next day, to start work on the book. I said she should call me if she needed anything. I gave her another packet of Zolpidem and made sure her phone was close at hand. We hugged.

With the traffic and pouring rain, it was almost nine by the time I got home. I was exhausted. I made myself a camomile tea with toast and sat in front of the TV. After an advert break came a new twist in the story: 'New evidence has shed light on Eduardo Ramelli's death. *News Today* has been able to establish that the author of *Happiness Is You* and *I Love Myself* was involved in a clandestine relationship with Karen Valdés (pictured), a prostitute allegedly implicated in the death of DEA agent John Toll, who died minutes after an encounter with the woman at the hands of a taxi driver who fled the scene, after robbing and shooting him. Toll had spent the night with the woman, who by day was a beautician in the prestigious salon, House of Beauty, located in Bogotá's Zona Rosa. She worked there until early today, when she was dismissed due to mental health issues and aggressive behaviour. Authorities are investigating possible connections between Valdés and the death of Ramelli and of John Toll, as well as the death, also in suspicious circumstances, of Sabrina Guzmán Paredes in the early hours of 23 July. Valdés was the last person to see the minor alive, as she had gone for a beauty treatment that afternoon. The bag stolen by the taxi driver contained valuable intelligence information. The DEA is working with Colombian authorities to clarify Karen Valdés's involvement in the crime. At the time of reporting, the whereabouts of the taxi driver is unknown.'

As the news went on, I felt a tightness in my chest. I'm not usually an impulsive person, but this time I didn't stop to think for even a second. As if I had spent my whole life preparing for this role, I jumped up from the sofa. I took my keys and handbag, and hurried out to the car. It was raining, like always. While I drove towards Karen's, I felt my heart beating wildly. The sleeping drug would help. It always did. One patient had confessed to her husband that she'd had a lover for the past five years. Then she had turned over and fallen asleep, like it was nothing. The next day, she got up, surprised not to find him by her side, having completely forgotten her confession. In a more drastic case, a man medicated with Zolpidem killed his mother last year in Bogotá. It happened everywhere, and in the best families. He himself was the one to call 123 the next day, shouting about reporting a murder. Someone had stabbed his mother! An investigation was initiated. The man was the first to be surprised by the findings. Paradoxically, he was found 'not guilty'. We usually believe that whoever commits a crime is guilty. And yet, being guilty requires an act of will. In this case, committing the crime and being guilty were two different things. The problem is that if this were applied to the law, we would pay less and less for our crimes and sins. We go around unconscious of our own impulses, desires and thought processes. We're shadows trapped in a cave.

The doorman opened the gate of the parking lot. He had seen me go in a few hours before with Karen.

'Go through, Doctor,' he said, as if he knew me. 'Remind me of your name, again?'

'Claire, Claire Dalvard.'

'Go on, it's 402.'

I took the lift. I had to press her doorbell again and again. Finally, Karen opened up. Her hair was in her face. Her eyes were open. She was smiling. I had no doubt she'd taken the pill. She was sleepwalking. She would answer any question honestly.

'Come in,' she said, her body rigid.

I sat down. After asking a few trivial questions – if she'd had dinner, what plans she had for the next day – I understood she was ready to respond on autopilot.

'Tell me something, how was John Toll's robbery arranged?'

I'd brought along the recorder I sometimes used for my patients' therapy sessions. I hit record.

'That was Wílmer.'

'Wílmer? Do you know his surname?'

'Delgado.'

'Had you been doing it a long time?'

'Doing it?' she asked. Then she started laughing.

'The robberies,' I said, trying not to lose the thread.

'No, not long, once or twice. He asked where I was and what time my client left, and I told him. I thought he was watching out for me. It was never the plan to hurt anyone. Never. I didn't know about the robberies.'

'But you wanted to help him?'

'He's married to my friend.'

'How many times did you give him a client's where-abouts after that?'

'Maybe four or five. He forced me to. He threatened to tell Maryuri about us. I didn't think …'

'Did you make victims withdraw money from ATMs?'

'I don't know about that. He only asked me what time my clients left after seeing me, and where that was.'

'And Eduardo?'

'What about him?'

'Were you seeing him for his money?' I asked.

'What money?' she said. 'The money that's in the case?'

With that, she curled up into a foetal position on the bed and fell fast asleep. I looked at her, then quickly searched in the obvious places. Under the bed was nothing. Then I opened the closet and there it was, a rigid, dark case. I opened it. Inside was an implausible amount of money, one-hundred-dollar notes in five-centimetre wads. I put it back, stood and left. The rain hadn't let up. On my way home, I couldn't help feeling a faint thrill. Suddenly I was the protagonist of this story. I could see clearly. I had missed the red flags. Like the addicts I treated, I felt I was in the grip of an epiphany. My empathy towards Karen had made me incapable of suspecting her. Perhaps because my view of her was condescending, filtered through pity, or through the guilt that hounds some of those of us who have everything. I was no more than a victim of my supposed superiority. I'd felt flattered to be the confidante of an unassuming beauty of modest means. My ego had kept me listening to her, seeking her out and offering her my help, never grasping that I was being manipulated. My supposed duty as a psychoanalyst was to remove the veil for my patients, that veil that we all carefully suspend between ourselves and the outside world. The distortion of reality shields us from suffering, but at the same time it can blindfold us.

My intuition had stopped being something I could trust. I saw in Karen a gentle person. Aware of even the slightest gesture. Well-rounded. Sharp. Thoughtful. Caring. Spontaneous. Good. And all of it was a deception. Karen was none other than a cold-blooded killer, a woman who did away with my friend's husband, who even had the audacity to tell me about one of her victims, playing the martyr. She won over my compassion and sold me a story completely counter to reality: Karen was no more than a hooker, corrupted by ambition to the point that she was capable of murdering for money.

I got home close to midnight. I decided not to call Lucía. I took a sleeping pill, closed my eyes. It was useless: I tossed and turned, got up, switched on the light, saw that it was two in the morning, took another sleeping pill, switched off the light, could only see Karen with her kind face, Karen talking about her son Emiliano, Karen dressed at first in clothing bought cheap in San Victorino, and months later in a fine coat, boots, a genuine leather handbag. How did I fail to realise? How didn't I see it earlier? Karen complaining about the bills she had to pay, Karen suffering, Karen hurting herself, Karen running her hand through her hair, Karen smiling, Karen sideways, her hand resting on her waist, Karen caressing my back, Karen arousing me, disturbing my good sense with her out-of-control sensuality. Her behaviour was textbook, it was as if I were a novice at this job. Karen was a sociopath; quite possibly she was capable of anything. No doubt the first time she saw me come into House of Beauty she thought, *Here's the person I need*. And so she pounced on me, I was her prey yet I didn't see it because Karen has a power and she knows it, her beauty is a weapon, that's why she looked at me as she did, that's why the touch of her hands sent shockwaves through my skin; I should have suspected our conversations, the laughs shared, the false complicity that grew within the cubicle. I turned on the light. It was already five, I had to sleep, I wasn't thinking straight. My mouth was claggy. I got up, poured a glass of water, drank it in great gulps, saw her face again, her child's face with the deep rings under the eyes, her crinkled brow as she heated the wax, her flat stomach, her pert breasts, her willowy body, her dimpled chin and her mouth – those pillowy lips, exquisite as a wild strawberry.

40.

When Luz woke me, my first patient had already arrived. I splashed water on my face, got dressed and hurried into the consulting room. I was exceedingly distracted, couldn't get Karen out of my head. I saw two more patients, and at midday got out my planner and called all patients scheduled that afternoon to cancel their appointments. Then I called the police and said I had information about the Toll case. They gave me another number and after much back and forth I was speaking with the prosecutor in charge. He said he'd just been assigned the case, after the previous prosecutor was promoted. It seemed as if he wanted it solved as soon as possible. He said he could see me in his office the same afternoon.

I quickly had lunch and drove my car there. The prosecutor was an older man. I wanted to know what had happened to the previous prosecutor. He didn't go into detail, said the orders had come from above. He couldn't say anything further.

Now I know I was acting out of spite, out of a desire for revenge. I felt betrayed, which is why I didn't stop to think about what I was doing. I was frank. I spoke for close to a quarter of an hour. I gave him the recording, as well as Karen's address. I explained where to find the suitcase. He promised my name would be kept out of it. I thanked him. I felt a certain relief, or I did for a short while, at least, because once I was in the car and headed home, the doubts started. The prosecutor's attitude didn't seem all that trustworthy. He had said, 'The working theory is that Karen hired someone to contact Sabrina via Facebook and arrange a date with her, with instructions to hurt her.' According to him, she did so because she was in love with Eduardo, who Sabrina was after.

'The typical story of a love triangle,' the prosecutor had added. The working theory? I asked myself. And who put forward such a theory? Who was behind that painstakingly pieced-together story about a 'love triangle'?

'Her colleagues at the salon back up the theory about her mental deterioration; there's no doubt she is, as you say, Doctor, an unstable person,' the prosecutor had insisted.

When I'd asked how he knew about the relationship between Sabrina Guzmán and Ramelli, the prosecutor had said it was 'an anonymous tip-off'. What if it was Diazgranados? What if he was behind a cover-up? I left the car in the basement and got into the lift. As soon as I reached my apartment, my phone rang. It was Lucía. I wasn't capable of answering. I asked Luz for a herbal tea, thought about getting into bed and trying to rest before doing anything else. On sitting down, I saw the flickering light of a message on the other side of the room. I went over to the telephone, hit the button and heard the voice of Consuelo Paredes saying she wanted to see me. 'Karen Valdés said to contact you. I've got information about Sabrina Guzmán's death. I'm her mother.' I called her back straight away. We agreed to meet an hour later at Il Pomeriggio. Time passed slowly. Time and again I went over what had happened in the past few days. Finally, I set off on foot. I found her sitting outside, wearing large, gold-framed sunglasses, her hair covering her face.

'Are you Claire?' she asked on seeing me.

'I am,' I said, 'how did you know?'

'I guess your appearance matches your name,' she said. She raised her sunglasses. She had deep rings under her red eyes. 'Pleased to meet you, I'm Consuelo Paredes.'

'Claire Dalvard.'

My hands were shaking. We were sitting near the water fountain. It had stopped raining but it was cold, a dry cold that seeped into the bones.

'Did Karen tell you about me?' I asked.

'She did. You look surprised.'

'A little. What did she say?'

'She said she trusted you.'

I felt my heart sinking.

'Claire, I think she's in danger. Look. I know they've changed the prosecutor in charge. I spoke to a forensics investigator. He explained that sometimes they do this when they want to manipulate the investigation.'

'I don't understand.'

'Someone wants to alter the course of an investigation, so they change the prosecutor in charge, as well as the people who make up the Technical Investigations Unit. They replace them with individuals who have already been bought off, with a prefabricated theory, a culprit, an alibi.'

'And who would be behind all this?' I asked, though I already knew the answer.

'Aníbal Diazgranados. Did you know he's the father of the person we think killed my daughter?'

'I had no idea,' I lied. 'But do you have any proof?'

'That's exactly what I wanted to talk to you about.'

The waiter came over. 'Ready to order?'

'A cappuccino for me,' said Consuelo Paredes.

'And I'll have a gin and tonic, please,' I said. 'You were saying?' My throat was dry.

'To cut a long story short, we hired a private detective who has a lot of experience. He found a note in Sabrina's bedroom signed L.A.D.'

'Luis Armando Diazgranados?'

'The very same. The investigator got a sample of the young man's handwriting and got a handwriting test done.'

'And did it come back positive?'

'It did,' said Consuelo Paredes.

'Is that proof enough to link him to your daughter's death?'

'We're going to try, though it looks like the new team in charge of the case is not going to consider it. They say it was obtained through illegal means, so it's invalid.'

'That can't be,' I said.

'My lawyer quit because they threatened to kill him. Claire, this is serious. Someone wants to frame Karen for the death of my daughter to cover Diazgranados's back.'

'What makes you think that?'

'My daughter's Facebook page was hacked. At least, that's what Cojack corroborated. It was done by the new investigation unit that has taken on the case. They want to fabricate evidence for the night she died.'

'Who is Cojack?'

'The detective.'

'His name is Kojak, like in the TV series?'

'Yes,' said Consuelo, impatiently.

'Okay,' I said, taking a long sip of gin. I had nothing to add.

'I expected more support from you, honestly. You don't seem that bothered. The only thing they need now to incriminate Karen for three homicides is binding proof. And in the meantime, Luis Armando walks free and so does the reprobate responsible for Toll's death. Do you realise they could extradite her? The DEA is behind this. The government wants to charge someone, and Karen will end up the scapegoat for Sabrina, Ramelli and Toll's deaths, even though she never laid a finger on any of them.'

I felt dizzy.

'You've gone pale,' said Consuelo. 'Are you feeling okay? Claire, don't you see? If Karen committed a crime, it was being an escort, but that's very different from being a killer!'

'And how do you know all this?'

'Cojack. He got in touch with Susana, a colleague of hers from the salon. She said Karen was an escort, that she was in a relationship with Wílmer Delgado, though she didn't know that he robbed Karen's clients or whether they had some kind of agreement, just that he had a taxi and was her friend's husband. She said she was positive Karen wasn't a criminal. The problem is, if Aníbal Diazgranados is behind this, it will be easy for him to link her to the other cases.'

'And the taxi driver, the one who took Sabrina to San Blas? You haven't looked for him?' I asked.

'Cojack had arranged to meet him at a billiards hall a few days ago. He never showed up. Then we found out that six days ago he was reported missing.'

'I have to go.'

'I'll pay,' said Consuelo curtly. She seemed annoyed. 'If you have to go, then go.'

'Do they have any proof to incriminate Karen?'

'They've got a video of her going into the motel with Toll. That does her damage, but doesn't prove she was involved in the murder. Personally, I don't think she was.'

'Then what do you think?'

'I think my daughter was her client at House of Beauty, then she got involved with Ramelli and the same with Wilmer, but never killed anyone.'

I kept quiet.

'But if there's no evidence, they can't incriminate her, can they?'

'Yes, they can. To send someone to jail, they need three things: cause, motive and opportunity. They've already built a case around that sacred trinity. And, corrupt as they are, don't be surprised if a piece of evidence suddenly appears.'

After a long silence searching for something to say, I got up with difficulty.

'Excuse me. I'm sorry not to be of more help. I have to go,' I said.

41.

Slowly I'm getting used to the smell of sweat, to carrying my tin and plastic cup along the corridor before dawn in search of breakfast, to the screams each time a woman gets her sentence, to the idea of a God who chokes but doesn't strangle, to the sad farewell parties when an inmate gets her freedom, to not seeing the moon or the stars, to not being able to drink a glass of water when I'm thirsty, to holding in the urge to urinate at the wrong time, to lining up to shit, eat and shower, to not sleeping. But I can't get used to this wish to die.

I'm writing because Claire asked me to. She finished writing her part of the book. Lucía is checking it over. Sometimes she makes a comment to add or delete something. They want me to read it to see if I think it's okay. No matter what it says, I'm not going to think it's okay. They say the book will help demonstrate my innocence. But it's already too late. Being locked in here made me guilty.

Since I've been here I've learned to read faces. Claire came again, once more loaded with apologies and presents, smelling of roses and lavender. I stared at her hands. She looked tired. She told me she's going back to

France; she couldn't find her feet in Colombia and feels like she can't do much for me. That's what she said. She said that a few days ago Luis Armando Diazgranados was shot in the middle of the day, on an ordinary street. I remembered Sabrina Guzmán and felt a momentary relief. I wondered who must be giving Claire her waxes, her massages.

Next week Lucía's coming to collect these pages. That's how we'll put a full stop to the book Claire wrote; to my story.

I don't care that my hearing was adjourned again. I don't care that Susana came to visit me, now married and pious, to tell me she forgives me. I'm never going to be able to cook like before, I don't want to think about the outside world any more. The outside world abandoned me, just as the desire to do anything has abandoned me, even writing to Emiliano. Those few desires have left me. I'd rather die locked up in here than have to go back out there.

I heard her the other night. The story is that once a woman hanged herself with her sheets, and the next day they found a red high heel hanging from her foot. From that day forward we haven't been allowed to use sheets, and they say that the woman in heels comes calling just before an inmate dies. At breakfast this morning, I told the women that I'd heard her. First, they didn't believe me. Then they bet on who'd be the next to die. Since I've been here, one woman has died. They say it's usually about two per year. Maybe that's another way to measure time. Maybe today the woman in heels will come for me. Maybe today will finally be my lucky day.